LOVE ALL OF ME

MOLLIE MATHEWS

For bees, the flower
is the fountain of life.
For flowers, the bee
is the messenger of love.

~ Kahlil Gibran,
The Prophet

ABOUT THIS BOOK

An unexpected lover...a volcano of exploding passions

AFTER SURVIVING a horrific accident Kate Miller is plagued by guilt. Hiding both her mental and physical scars, she shuns love and escapes into work—finding meaning and purpose in running her boutique Manuka honey business.

Billionaire business magnate, Gianni Romano has ventured to New Zealand driven by the crimes of his father and the memories he wants to escape. But the infamous Romano name and ill-gained fortune follow him wherever he goes. But this only makes the headstrong Italian more determined to strike out on his own. Now he's on the cusp of achieving world acclaim.

Only one woman stands in his way—fiercely independent Kate Miller and her refusal to submit to his demands that she sells her business to him. Her passions are inflamed. How dare he think he can flaunt his considerable wealth and buy the only thing that gives her a reason to live?

The spark they have is hotter than a Sicilian sunset and conflict flames. When emotions run deep and hearts are on the line will mixing business with pleasure be the bedrock for a lifelong love? Or will their love explode like an angry volcano?

Love All of Me is a beautiful romance, brimming with the promise of a happily ever after. Set in The Bay of Islands, New Zealand—one of the most beautiful, unspoiled, sensuous places in the world.

JOIN MOLLIE'S READERS GROUP:)
    https://www.facebook.com/groups/323525616931811

1

"I never thought it would happen to me." Kate Miller looked down at the picture art therapist Issy Riley had asked her to draw. Issy's instructions had been simple, 'Just draw what you feel.'

Kate hadn't known where to begin and then in a mindless blur all the hurt, all the pain, all the grief, flew from her fingers in frenzied crayon scrawls.

Her fingers clenched the hard black crayon as she glanced

down at her scribbles. There on the page in an incoherent blur were all those memories Kate thought she had talked through until she was bruised and blue. All those toxic thoughts that she thought she had healed. All those terrifying traumas she thought she had pushed so far to the back of her mind had exploded through.

Kate rubbed her hand below her abdomen feeling the puckered ridge of the scars and skin grafts she covered up and hid from the rest of the world. Physical scars she hid from view, not unlike the way she tried to hide her mental scars.

It had been a year since the fatal day that had detonated her happiness. For nearly 12-months she had plastered on a brave face of self-reliance.

But now it was a week before Christmas and everything had erupted to the surface. She was so terrified of the consequences she reached out for help.

Kate studied the black sooty image, forged with thick crayoned blazes of black and frenzied scribbles of grey and grimaced. She lifted her hand to the thick fringe of flame-coloured hair, and pressed it down against her forehead, feeling as she did so the indentations and scars caused by flying volcanic rock.

"I don't know if this is a good idea," Kate's voice was thick with conviction and intensity. Her mood had changed since entering the therapist's room. She was at once furtively angry and coolly clear in her certainty that mining her emotions was a big mistake.

"Use a new page if you like," Issy said.

Her tone was so compassionate and kind and Kate instantly trusted her. Kate had worked with a great number of therapists since the accident and not one of them seemed to truly care. And she liked that Issy was creative and unconventional. She sensed she was a nonconformist, an outsider, just like Kate.

"Feel free to edit," Issy handed Kate a pair of scissors. "Cut out anything that you don't like. Anything that you don't want. Anything you want to change," Issy said changing her words, as though being careful not to lead Kate too much or direct where Kate's subconscious wanted to go.

Kate looked at the pad of paper balanced on a board on her knees and tore off a sheet of paper. She grabbed the glue stick Issy handed her and pasted it over her memories, then slapped the fresh page down.

"How do you feel?" Issy asked.

Blank.

That's what Kate felt.

Blank and empty and nothing, she affirmed silently as her gaze sunk into the white void. A void just like the gaping hole in her life where her family used to be.

"Better," Kate lied. She clenched her fist and forced it to the page and rubbed it back and forth in vigorous sweeps over the paper. She knew she should confide in the therapist but the truth was she didn't want to lift the lid off the emotions she strove so hard to suppress.

She didn't want to tell Issy 'I feel nothing, and that's how I want it.' She feared, just like the volcano on White Island that had erupted that awful day, once her feelings exploded to the surface they would prove fatal.

She raked her hands through her hair. God, she was just hanging on as it was. Every semblance of her life that she had scraped together hung by a tiny worn thread. Every tiny little morsel of the reason why she kept on living was reduced to stale crumbs. Every tear she stuffed down threatened to hurl itself onto the page. And she was terrified that once she lifted the lid on the guilt that consumed her every waking moment would explode. Because all she wanted to do was die.

Kate glanced at the clock on the therapist's wall. Three minutes to three. Three her lucky number. Or, rather it had been. Three minutes more until her session would be over.

Thank God.

She was stupid to think that this would change anything, but she wanted to try. Didn't she owe it to Zac? Didn't she owe it to her bees? Didn't she owe it to—she gulped hard, suddenly feeling she couldn't breathe—didn't she owe it to her dad?

She was sick of living like this. Unable to feel. Dead from the heart down, permanently scarred and terrified of the dark thoughts that permeated her mind like the sulphurous gas and toxic fumes that killed so many people that hateful day.

She clenched her eyes as the video footage of the burns many victims suffered replayed in her mind. No, she affirmed, pushing the truth away. Her parents had died from the fumes, she silently affirmed, not wanting to think the worse.

"It's okay to cry, Kate," Issy said, handing her a tissue. "You can't always be stoic. Tears tell truths. Tears are healing."

Kate shook her head. She didn't want to accept the truth and she didn't deserve to heal. "I'm fine," she said. *I am a rock.*

"Why did you come here, Kate?" Issy gently probed.

Kate shrugged. "I thought coming back to New Zealand would be therapeutic. You know sort of like face the fear and—"

She bit her lip. That was the problem. She had faced the fear. It had been her idea. Her whole family, at Kate's insistence, had faced the fear of the awakening volcano and look where it had got them.

Dead.

Issy looked at her sympathetically. "I meant, here, here," she said, sweeping her hands around the counselling room.

Kate turned away. She shouldn't have come. She didn't want sympathy. She didn't want kindness. And she most definitely didn't want people worrying about her. She had a hard enough job worrying about herself. And now she was worrying about being a failure counselling client. Issy deserved a more pliant client.

There you go again, she cursed under her breath, getting stuck in your old paradigm of worrying for everyone else.

And then the truth splintered through her mind. The fact was if she'd done a better job worrying about everyone else she wouldn't have nagged her family to go on the volcanic excursion.

She blamed herself and no amount of therapy was ever going to change the facts.

Christmas last year her mum, dad, and sister—her whole family—died. She had killed them. And on that day she swore she would never care or love anyone again.

Issy glanced at the clock. "I'm sorry, Kate, but I have another client. Are you okay if we leave things there for today?"

Kate nodded. "Sure."

"Same time next week?"

"Yes, same time next week is perfect," she lied. She wouldn't be coming back. Ever. Without her family what was the point in living?

2

"Thanks for waiting, Zac," Kate said, as she opened the driver's door of the ute. "Now slide over."

Zac pretended not to hear and kept his nose pressed against the top of the steering wheel.

"Zac, move over. Come on. If you could drive, I'd let you. But I hate to break it to you, you're a dog. And dog's can't drive. It's the law."

He regarded her with determined dark eyes, then turned, and padded to the passenger side.

"You know I love you," she said, sweeping her hand

vigorously across his fur. The truth was if it wasn't for Zac and her bees Kate wouldn't be here at all. She loved her rescue dog more than life itself. And her bees gave her something of her father to hang onto. A calling. They needed her. They gave her a reason to live.

She clenched the steering wheel, and eye-balled the roof, willing her tears not to flow. Not here. Not now. *What right did she have to cry?*

Because of Kate, her mum, and her dad, and her sister had left the safety of the cruise ship and joined a tour to the volcano on White Island—and now they were dead.

Kate looked back at Zac. Zac looked back at Kate, just as he had that day she had rescued him, death in his eyes. Only now she knew he was faking it to get his way.

Zac was not the dog she thought she would choose when she went to the animal centre a year ago.

She had wanted a happy, bouncy puppy, one that would be self-reliant—just like her. A puppy that would make her feel better. But on his best day with his sad brown eyes, and jet-black coat, he looked like a professional mourner. And in the end, that had suited her fine.

Nobody had wanted a three-legged, pug dog with a skin impediment. And she couldn't have left him in the animal rescue centre. Not once she found out that the day she had called in was to be his last day.

She patted his soft, sleek fur. The eczema had flared because Zac had been so poorly treated. And she knew, with love, unlike her own scars, Zac's would heal. Everyone needed to be loved. She needed to be loved. And now she had someone to love too.

She had Zac.

Zac.

He had not been the man she had dreamed she would

spend her life loving. He had not been the man she had dreamed she would have children with. He had not been the man she had vowed she would marry. . .

. . .until—'Til death would they part.

Kate sucked a big gulp of air forcing the grief and pain through her chest and gently pressed Zac's nose. Zac had been Prozac with three legs and a short, stump of a tail. He had saved her life.

"We have a lot in common you and me. You knew I couldn't leave knowing I could've saved you and didn't."

Zac rolled his eyes up to stare at her, and moved back to the driver's seat, plunking himself in Kate's lap.

"I saved your butt, now move your pudgy arse," she said, nudging him. "Pretty please, Zac, move back. I'll be late for the beautician."

Zac grunted and stumbled into the passenger seat. He hobbled around and around as he situated himself on the split tan upholstery.

"Don't look so depressed, you're supposed to cheer me up—not make me feel guilty."

Zac didn't get much happier as they drove away from the counselling rooms. Instead, he stared wistfully at her lap.

"Okay come on then," she said patting her thighs. Zac didn't wait to be asked twice. Zac met her eyes, and plunged toward her, licking her from chin to brow with sweeping slurps.

Kate burst into tears. "Oh, Zac," she sobbed wrapping an arm around him. His body was warm and wriggly and welcoming. Kate held him tighter, so thankful to have someone to hold in her life. Especially at Christmas when she felt so sad.

"It's just me and you, Zac," she told him, tears running down her cheeks.

Zac sighed and began to lick the salty droplets, which made Kate cry even harder.

She wrapped her arms around his pudgy belly. She felt sad and happy at the same time. It was a relief to cry after holding everything in for so long. She gave one final sniff and let go of him.

"I have to get myself together before anyone sees my tears," she said. "And I can't be late for the beautician."

Balancing on one leg Zac pressed his paws on the window ledge and smeared the glass with his squishy nose.

"Okay, but no leaping out when you see a pretty girl," Kate said, pressing the button and lowering the window.

"You are family now, Zac," she told him. "And I'm not losing anyone else again."

3

"That was a big one." Kate clenched her hand around the padded metal tube encased in padding and grimaced as Christmas songs played through the beauty therapist's room.

'*All I want for Christmas is you,*' crooned Mariah Carey and Justin Bieber. An image of Kate's mum and dad and sister fluttered before her clenched eyes. She grimaced and gripped the handle harder, focusing attention on the river of pain as it ruptured her chin, willing herself to feel the intensity of the electric current and the sting. The sting, the hurt, the pain—anything but the torrent of grief engulfing her heart.

Mariah and Justin continued their duet completely devoid of any knowledge of why Christmas sucked.

'I don't care about the presents
Underneath the Christmas tree.
I just want you for my own.
More than you could ever know.
Make my wish come true.
All I want for Christmas is you.'

A salty trickle trailed from Kate's eyes. It had been a year and she had never cried in front of anyone but Zac. Why here? Why now? Why the f**k?

"Are you okay?" the therapist asked. "Do you want me to stop?"

"No," Kate said too quickly and too loudly.

"Are you sure?"

Kate nodded.

"Maybe I struck a nerve," the therapist said.

Kate shook her head. She wanted to tell her that the only thing striking her nerves was the far too joyful music hailing through the room.

'Laughter fills the air
And everyone is singing
I hear those sleigh bells ringing
Santa won't you bring me
The one I really need.'

KATE SHOULD HAVE JUST BEEN honest about how the music was making her feel. She should have told the beauty therapist that she tensed as the music seeped into every cell, every memory, every fibre of hair that now stood erect on her skin in a state of shock.

She should have confided that the stupid cheesy Christmas songs were more excruciating than the jarring jolts of electrical current from the electrolysis. But she couldn't say that. She couldn't even wipe away the wayward tears without attracting attention. The only thing she could do was to get the hell out of there.

"I'm sorry," Kate said, pulling off her eye-pad and unclenching the rod she gripped in her fingers. She flung it over the side of the bed.

"I can't. . .I just can't. . .I have to go." She swung her legs over the bed, stood up, plunged her feet into her sandals and paced across the room. Tears blurred her vision as she threw open the door and sprinted through the reception area. She yanked the door to the salon open. Not wanting to see or talk to anyone. Wanting only to escape to the solitude of her bee farm and home.

The brightness of the daylight blinded Kate as she stepped onto the street. She turned, remembering she hadn't paid for her electrolysis.

Boom! She walked, chin-first, with a thud into a far too firm, far too rock-hard, far too muscular chest.

Her face plunged into fire engine red velvet. She folded momentarily into the strangely comforting fabric. He felt soft, yet hard; friendly yet firm; tender yet tough. Awareness jolted through her.

"Well, that's one way to get Santa's attention," said the inhabitant of the red hot suit. His Italian-tinged tone held a trace of the exotic, she mused momentarily savouring the sultry texture of his voice. A trill of uninvited desire laced down her spine as the potent masculinity of his accent coiled around her.

And then her eyes met his. Tawny-gold, the colour of molten fire. His gaze surveyed her with unsparing assessment. Kate stiffened as though she'd been measured, judged, and found wanting.

"Perhaps you'd prefer to sit on my knee," Santa said, his voice, crisply mocking, with its fascinating slight accent, slashed across Kate's startled silence.

"I most certainly would not!" she threw at him, wanting to rid him of his amused enjoyment as he feasted on her mortified surprise.

Heart juddering against her breastbone, she sprung back. Although Kate had intended to run away without giving him the satisfaction of her second glance, her gaze flicked up. To her chagrin, she was captured by eyes gleaming with sardonic derision. The bold warrior's face hardened into ruthlessness, yet a misplaced flare lightened the golden depths of his gaze.

She tossed her tresses of amber hair in feigned nonchalance and looked away lest he see the tears still pooling in her eyes. He was not the fat ruddy-faced Santa she was accustomed to. He was not the naturally plump local who volunteered for the role of Father Christmas for the past 11 years. *He was not her Santa.*

He was far too sexy. Far too masculine. Far too dangerous.

He was a sex symbol with a physique worthy of gracing a nude male calendar and he knew it, Kate thought to her annoyance. His 6ft-3inch frame towered over her. She could tell, despite his head-to-toe Santa masquerade that he was one of those rare figures like Muhammad Ali who emerged once a generation. Athletic, intelligent, arrogant deliciously charismatic.

Infinitely dangerous.

And then the Oxford-educated accent with a load of Italian decadence spoke again, "Have you been a good girl?"

No, she hadn't been a good girl. So he could get lost. And she would tell him so. She turned and braced herself for confrontation. But instead of assaulting him with her full defiance, she melted into his looks. He was arrestingly handsome with bed-roomy eyes, and run-your fingers-though-my-tousled liquorice-black hair peeking beneath his Santa's hat and snow-white wig.

He was everything Kate didn't need. *And didn't deserve.* And even if she did consider a harmless bit of hot-Santa fun, which she so wouldn't, he was looking at her as though he owned her. She would not, could not, give him the satisfaction of what he was sure to think would be an easy conquest.

Damn you, she affirmed silently to her traitorous body as a rivet of electricity shot up her legs. Blood flamed through her body, sending a flushed feeling at the base of her throat as she felt the heat of 5000 volts pulsing through her.

He is a mere mortal, she affirmed. Not a God. Not my saviour. A callous, unfeeling, arrogant man masquerading as kindness. If looks could kill, she mused, summoning her most murderous look, he'd already be dead.

Dead. What a horrible thing to wish on anyone. What's wrong with you, she wondered as guilt threw water on her determination to be rid of him and the treacherous desire that ran through her body.

"Kate, you left without paying."

Kate turned to see the beautician leaning out of the store, her foot wedged between the door.

"Oh, yes, I'm sorry…I—" she mumbled. Embarrassment and relief stomped through her body. She shoved her flame-coloured hair behind her ears, pulled her shoulders back, and grabbed her purse from the leather bag slung over her shoulders.

As Kate stepped back inside and slipped her debit card into the machine, from deep in her memory she heard her father's voice. 'Sometimes life has a funny way of throwing fate in your face.' It was a theme he had instilled in her when she was just a girl—to always look on the light side of life.

The unexpected memory spiked through her heart. Kate could imagine her father laughing and laughing, watching as the daughter who vowed never to love again crashed breasts-to-chest into Santa—the man everyone loved. But not just any Santa. Arguably the best looking Santa on the globe.

Centrefold Santa.

Anyone but him, she thought. She wasn't sure why she found him so threatening. She just knew that she did. He unnerved her, threw her, challenged her in a way no man had ever succeeded.

His gaze trawled over the length of her lithe body clad in a black tee-shirt and ink-black jeans, before returning to her sombre face. "Has somebody died?" he asked in a hard, uncompromising, very nearly ruthless tone.

Kate was stunned. Frozen momentarily in a mix of horror and fury. "You've got to be joking," she fired. "What sort of sick arse are you?"

She turned and walk briskly back to her ute. Muttering and cursing and vowing never to think of him again. Against her will she found herself looking back. Looking back at his lean and muscled form visible beneath the sleek stain of his Santa suit. Looking back at the feelings the collision had fired in her.

All she could see was red. Not the red of danger. Not the red of stop. But a sultry red—the colour and texture and scent of something—*someone*—more exciting. *Ferrari red. The colour of passion and go, go, go.*

What the hell was wrong with her?

4

Kate dived into the safety of her ute, slid Zac to the passenger side, and slammed the door shut. She turned the key in the ignition. She grimaced as the radio chimed:

> *Sleep in heavenly peace. . .*
> *the infant so tender and . . .*

She pushed the dial and turned it off. Leaning her head on the steering wheel she suppressed a sob. She would never have children. Never be a besotted mother. Never feel a husband's love. Her parents would never be grandparents. Her sister would never be an aunt.

And she would never allow herself to love as long as she lived. What was the point? Why had she been spared? She wasn't living. She was waiting to die.

Zac shuffled onto her knees and looked up at her with wide, dark, silently beseeching eyes. 'What about me? Will you always love me?' he appeared to plead.

"Don't guilt-trip me," she sobbed, rubbing the soft, plump folds under his neck.

Change.

To change my reality all I have to do is change my thoughts," she said to Zac as the words from Dr Joe Dispenza's book, *Breaking The Habit of Being Yourself,* ripped through her mind.

"It's easy for Dr Joe to say that," she told Zac. "He has everything. Everyone he loves is alive." But then Kate reminded herself of Dr Joe's story. How, following a freak cycling accident, he had nearly died. How he was told he would be paralysed. How people told him he'd have to close his chiropractic business. How everything looked bleak. But then Dr Joe used the power of his mind.

But Kate's mind couldn't be trusted. Her traitorous brain couldn't get rid of the fire engine red Santa she'd left pacing outside the beautician's rooms. Santa looked like he should be on an Armani billboard advertising underwear. Not on the rural streets of small-town Kerikeri—the largest town in The Bay of Islands, population 5000. What was

Centrefold Santa doing here? Why had he invaded her thoughts?

She drove the 11 kilometres from the town centre and headed home.

Quit thinking about him, she said as she got out of her ute. Taking Zac in her arms, she strode to the shed where she kept all her bee-keeping gear and placed him at her feet. She kicked off her boots and thrust her legs into her white vented bee-suit. She yanked it over her thighs, then plunged her feet back into her boots, stomping the dry earth with extra conviction.

No Santa, no matter how gorgeous, was going to distract Kate from a hard day's work. She clenched her hands and fisted them through the long sleeves. She folded the veiled hood over her head. After doing a safety check to make sure all zippers and hook and loop closures were properly sealed, she placed her hands into her gloves.

As she walked around the back of the shed toward the beehives, Kate suddenly remembered the words her father had said. 'Bees only sting you if your heart is impure.' Her father had joked that he was always being stung. But he never was.

A swarm of guilt stung her thoughts as she recalled the way she had lashed out at Red Hot Santa. How was he to know her family had been killed in the White Island volcano disaster last Christmas? How was he to know that she had lost her whole family? Centrefold Santa had not meant to taunt her when he asked if someone had died, Kate thought as she lifted the hives onto the back tray.

She drove through the paddocks with the bees on the back of her ute to take them to a fresh patch of Manuka for the bees to sit amongst. She slowed the ute to a stop and clambered out of the truck and walked around to the back.

She lifted the blue and yellow and pink hives from the tray and placed them on the ground. The hives, painted in colours that attracted the bees and helped them find their way home to the correct hive, were a cheery reminder of the power of colour to nurture and heal.

She began to wonder if she hadn't been keeping herself imprisoned in her black, funeral clothes for too long—depriving herself of joy and punishing herself for surviving.

Kate recalled the words Issy had said during their counselling session, 'Just notice your feelings and allow them to move through you. Do not suppress, or silence the pain, or numb it in any way. But just watch and observe. Feelings are like ripples drifting across a river.'

Kate looked over at the pond and lost her thoughts momentarily as she studied the reflections of the plump volumes of clouds gliding across the soft blue water. Only yesterday they had only reminded her of the smoky plumes of ash that had filled the sky in the days following the eruption.

Now instead of seeing only haunting reminders of what she had lost for some reason she couldn't put her gloved finger on, she saw clouds shaped like love hearts.

Big plump love hearts. Floating directly above her. Another cloud was shaped like two big hearts united as one. Like the huge, heaving heart in her body that was now pumping with blood as she thought about her run in with Centrefold Santa.

She pushed the thoughts to one side. She didn't want to feel those feelings. She didn't want them to drift through her body. She wanted to stuff them down.

She watched as the bees began to fly through the air. They didn't fly solo. The bees flew as a community. Together, buzzing happily, nothing worrying them.

She wondered for a moment how bees felt when some of them died. Maybe they don't feel anything, she thought. Maybe there was something to learn from the bees. Perhaps there was protection and comfort in their community because they still had the company of others, she wondered.

Kate's phone rang and she reached into her pocket and lifted it to her ear.

"Hi Kate, it's Jacqui."

"I know, Jacqui. You're my best friend. Your number is programmed in my phone."

"Am I bothering you?"

"No, I'm just out with Zac and the bees."

"Zac and your bees. Don't you think it's time you got a real boyfriend?"

"I don't have time for a boyfriend. My bees are busy. They don't stop for a break. And Zac needs me."

"I know this isn't your thing… " Jacqui said. "I know you don't do Christmas…I'll understand completely …it's just…I wouldn't ask…"

"Ask what?"

"If I wasn't in a bind."

"What? It sounds serious."

"It is, and it isn't. It's serious and it's not."

"What? Can you just tell me?"

"Well, you know with the fires in Australia. . .everyone is swamped. They need extra medics. Especially for the children. There are so many kids who have been—" Jacqui paused, then continued, choosing her words carefully. "—so many people have been caught in the fires. I need to go to Australia. Tonight."

"Wow! I didn't realise it was so serious. Of course, you have to go. We can get by."

"No, it's not that. It's—well, I promised. . ."

"Promised what?"

"I promised to be Santa's helper."

5

Kate's breath caught in her chest. She knew what was coming before Jacqui uttered her plea.

"Can you be Santa's helper?"

Kate leaned against a tree and twisted her foot in the soil. "Maybe Santa's flying solo this year," Kate said.

"Santa doesn't do single. He always has a helper. Someone to help him give kisses and cuddles and gifts to the children. The kids look forward to it. It's the highlight of the year. A lot of these children have nothing. They come from poor homes. They have no money, no food, no presents.

Nothing. Santa's helper shares the load, picking up and distributing food and toys with Santa.'

"I guess, he'll have to find another helper," Kate said.

"That's the thing. It's why I'm calling."

I'll do anything, just don't ask me to do that, Kate prayed inwardly. *Not with him.*

"Kate, will you help me out? Will you be Santa's helper?"

Kate groaned. "Who's Santa?" she asked praying inwardly Jacqui would confirm it wasn't Centrefold Santa.

"I'm not sure. Probably one of the old guys from the retirement home. Why?"

"No reason," Kate lied. She should've told Jacqui about her run-in with Adonis but she knew Jacqui would be like Zac with a bone, chasing the impossible, feasting on the idea that her best friend would have a fairytale Christmas romance.

"One of the oldies from the retirement home? Are you absolutely sure?" Kate asked again.

"It's been that way for the last three years. I can't think who else would volunteer."

Kate crushed the ground with her boots.

I can.

"Sure. For you Jacqui, anything." She prayed the slopping in her gut warning her of danger was less about her morbid fear that Santa was the adonis she had face-planted and more about the pie she'd eaten for lunch.

"Thanks, Kate. You're a lifesaver."

"No. Jacqui. I'm not," she mumbled under her breath.

"I'll leave the outfit at my place. Can you swing by and pick it up?"

'What do I need to do?" Kate said, groaning inwardly.

"They're loading up Santa's ute tonight and then you'll be driving out to the Maori settlements.

"Santa drives?"

"It's 2020 Kate. Of course, Santa drives. The kids all know he comes early in his ute. The bigger kids tell the little ones that Santa will fly across the sky on Christmas morning to check that they're having an awesome day. For now, he wants to swing by and say hello and see if they have any special wishes and give a few early presents to the good kids."

* * *

"I HATE CHRISTMAS," Kate said to Zac as she opened Jacqui's door with her spare key. "But I'm going to try. For the kids."

On the hall table neatly folded in a blaze of satin red was her outfit. Her tiny, weeny, super teeny costume, she realised with horror as she inspected it.

Zac cocked his head to one side and frowned. Taking the lead he padded to Jacqui's bedroom and barked.

"Okay. Okay. I get it," Kate said. "The sooner we start the sooner we can go home." She scooped up the silky nightmare and joined Zac.

She kicked off her boots and thrust her feet through the satin opening and hitched the dress over her boobs. Then yanked on the small white fringed cape. At least her shoulders wouldn't be exposed, and if she pulled it tightly she could cover her chest.

Just.

Kate tightened the belt, clinching it tight around her narrow waist. Then pulled on the candy-striped stockings, pulling them high to the top of her thigh and repositioned the little satin bows. Then thrust her feet into the ridiculously high black boots, fringed with white fur.

"This is going to be gruelling," she muttered as she pulled the little Santa hat over her hair. "This outfit could only just pass for a general audience," she said looking in the bedroom mirror. "If the skirt rode any higher, or the bustier fell any lower I'd look like an x-rated adult movie star. How is this even suitable for kids?"

Zac barked his agreement.

"Don't look so smug," Kate said, "Look there's a little elf suit for you."

Zac rolled on his back.

"Playing dead isn't going to cut it," Kate said.

Brushing back the flood of gently waving, silky amber hair, she pulled a face at her reflection.

"Christmas can't be over soon enough."

"Christmas is hot this year," a sultry, uncomfortably familiar voice purred as Kate stepped out of the ute.

She looked up, mortified, as his gaze trawled the length of Kate's thigh as the skirt snagged on the buckle of her seatbelt. Proud lion-like eyes combed over her body in primal appreciation, then lifted to her face.

Her worst nightmare had come true.

Pulling her dress free, Kate perched precariously on the ridiculous heels, thrusting her shoulders back in an attempt to convey absolute control.

"Northland is always hot at Christmas," she said, cooly.

Leonardo Bressolini grinned. "Gianni, this is Kate. Kate meet Gianni. She'll be riding you—riding with you," he corrected.

Gianni chuckled. Not a quiet chuckle, but a big, deep gritty chuckle that swarmed all over her.

Gianni. Of course, he'd have a glamorous playboy's name to match this infantile behaviour. And of course Leonardo, the showy millionaire water magnate who had now made The Bay of Islands his home would be the one to throw them together.

"It will be my pleasure to ride you," Gianni said, lathering on the sultry accent.

Kate brought all her willpower to bear, ruthlessly quashing the images her treacherous brain supplied far too eagerly.

"I am not a toy to amuse you," she snapped, twisting away from him.

"What's got into you? You're acting like an old married couple," Leonardo said, as he piled a giant doll and other toys into the waiting ute.

Gianni gestured an apology with his hands. No, not an apology, it was a denial, Kate decided, as Gianni held his hands in the air and stepped back in a gesture of peace. Despite the space, sparks burned between them.

"Oh, before I forget," Leonardo said, passing her a lipstick. "Your friend Jacqui called in on her way to the airport. She left this for you."

"What am I supposed to do with this?" Kate asked, looking at the slender capsule in horror.

"Well, you're not going to eat it for starters," Leonardo said. "Gianni, you know the delicate sensitivities of women's lips. Can you give your helper a hand?"

Kate clamped her mouth shut and crossed her arms over her chest. "I don't wear makeup," she protested. "But I can assure you I'm quite capable. *I am a capable, competent person.*"

"It has to be done perfectly. One false move, one misstep, one slip and your mouth will look like a blood bath. Do you want to terrify the kids?" Gianni said.

"Of course I don't."

"Then don't be so stubborn."

Gianni lifted a long sensuous finger and pressed it to her mouth. Raising her top lip, her mouth parted like a flower stimulated by the promise of a bee's proboscis.

Taking the tube in his fingers Gianni glided the sultry red wax on her lips, applying it in long, fluid movements as he explored Kate's traitorous mouth.

Unbearably aroused, melting with a confusing mix of desire and mortification, she forced her lips into a tight line. But Gianni would not be deterred. With erotic skill he slid the lipstick with the intimate prowess of a lover claiming a virgin for the first time, opening her with his touch, exploring her vulnerable flesh with scorching purpose.

Kate moaned slightly, every movement of his body escalating the wickedly agonising pleasure that swam through her until all she wanted was for him to finish what he'd started.

"*I saw Mommy kissing Santa Claus. Underneath the mistletoe last night*" Leonardo sang. Laughing, he lifted a plastic piece of mistletoe and flung it at them.

Gianni lowered his face toward her. Leaning in, he lifted his finger and drew it along the edge of her lip, as though wiping an errant line of colour.

He drew his finger to his mouth and placed it on his lips as though he was tasting her scent. Then in a moment of supreme control, he leaned in and took Kate's mouth, kissing her deeply, powerfully, intimately, as the first ripple of need quaked through her body.

"Get a room." Leonardo laughed.

But they were powerless to stop. Their tongues united in a blaze of desire. Gianni's sultry eyes pinned her like a hypnotic spell, as her lips contracted around his and dragged her over the edge of control.

Deeper and deeper she fell, losing all rational self-control. She'd never felt anything like it, the whole experience a shattering revelation about her capacity for sensuality. It was as dangerous as it was exciting.

She was barely cognisant of the growing crowd of locals drawing closer to them. It was only when someone's cellphone chimed the lyrics to a Cindy Lauper song that reality dawned.

AND GIRLS, they wanna have fun
  Oh, girls just wanna have fun...
  The phone rings, in the middle of the night
  My father yells "What you gonna do with your life?"
  Oh, daddy dear, you know you're still number one
  But girls they wanna have fun
  Oh, girls just wanna have. . .
  Fun.

SUDDENLY, without warning, anger exploded in her chest, and the far too good looking hunk, who thought himself superior, was her target.

"What the hell are you doing?" she hissed at him, pushing him away. She glared at his chiselled cheekbones and golden-toned skin. *You think you can take what you want.*

He stared at her with blank, slack-jawed, amusement. *"Kissing Santa's helper, babe."*

"I live here. Everyone will talk. And don't call me babe. I am not your babe."

"You're right. I'm sorry. How inconsiderate of me. I should have ignored the mistletoe. Allowed you to refuse me and accepted the bad luck that would have rained upon us because of the mistletoe curse. All because you've cancelled fun this Christmas."

"Fun! That wasn't fun. That was humiliating," she threw at him.

A bemused smile grazed Gianni's formidable lips as he sat behind the wheel. His gaze met hers in a moment of recognition.

Did he understand her pain? Did he sense her hurt? A gnawing sense of premonition collided with a torrent of anger and fear surging through her body in a maelstrom of opposing currents.

She felt guilty and excited; afraid and exhilarated; happy and sad. Every conflicting emotion collided through her body, reducing her to a quivering mess.

She wanted to be alone—she dreamed of sharing her life.

She wanted to be independent—she dreamed of someone to rely on.

She wanted—

She closed her eyes and clenched them shut. God, she didn't know what she wanted anymore. All she knew was she never wanted to hurt like she had when everyone she loved had died.

She was a mess, Kate affirmed, as she registered the crowd gathered around the ute. *And the whole tiny town knew it.*

She grabbed Zac from her ute and placed him on the back

seat. She climbed into the Land Rover laden with presents. Had she cancelled Christmas? Would it be so wrong to have a little bit of fun?

7

"What was that about?"Kate braced herself against the front seat and scowled as Gianni slid his six-foot-three-inch frame into his pewter grey Land Rover.

"You tell me," Gianni said, turning the key in the ignition.

She leaned forward and grabbed the rearview mirror and twisted it toward her.

"Look at my face" she cried, trying to rub away the red lipstick smeared over the edges of her lips.

"How was I to know you'd be such a sloppy kisser?" he said, running the back of his hand over his mouth.

"You kissed me," Kate said.

"You kissed me back."

Zac perched between them. His head twisted from one to the other as he enjoyed the volley of blame.

"I look like a bee's stung me," Kate said, thrusting a finger on her swollen lips.

"I was helping you."

"Yeah right," she said, as he turned off the highway "Helping yourself to the honey, more like," she muttered.

The back of the Range Rover fishtailed as he pulled onto the dusty gravel.

Kate gripped the armrest. "Avoid reality if you want to but don't run us off the road," she said through wind-blown hair that caught in her mouth as she spoke. "I had hoped you could drive better than you kiss," Kate said dizzily as she savoured the tingle that hadn't stopped since he'd claimed her mouth in his.

"Don't give up your day job. Actually, what is your day job? What do you do when you're not pretending to be a kind, gentle, completely trustworthy Santa?"

"I'm an acquirer," Gianni said.

"Which is English for what?" Kate asked.

"I see things I want and I get them," he said.

"Do you always succeed?"

"Yes."

Rather than irritate her, his unflinching confidence reassured Kate. He clearly had an incisive mind and judging from the superbly sleek, maritime blue Rolex on his wrist he wasn't short of a dime.

"And you? What is it you do?" Gianni asked. Like his

watch he oozed the seriousness and physicality and potent danger of James Bond.

Kate pressed her lips together. Now he was being nosy. She didn't want to tell him about her bee colony. She wanted to keep that to herself. Just like she wanted to keep herself to herself. Besides, she wouldn't be seeing him again once the Santa trip was over, so there wasn't any point telling him any more about herself then she needed. Distance equalled safety, she avowed.

"What are you avoiding?" He asked after a lengthy silence. "Catherine Miller?" he summoned, tasting the fullness of her name.

The back of her neck prickled. She sucked in a breath as she turned. "I'm not avoiding *anything*," she bit. *I'm avoiding you.*

"You're angry," his tawny eyes glittered with magnetic energy and she felt it. Everywhere.

Kate wanted to confide in him, 'You're wrong. I'm not angry. I'm sad. I'm so sad, I'm mad. And I'm especially mad with myself for kissing you. But more than that, I'm mad because I want to do it again. And sad, because I'm afraid I'll only get hurt.

So why then, was it so dammed hard to quench the heat that blazed between them? The sensual possession of his mouth had summoned a fire that stirred her soul. Searing through the debris and accretions of the past year. His kiss had stripped every bit of numb weariness from her, casting her back into the adolescent turmoil of her first crush, the year she had turned sixteen.

"Your brusqueness is astonishing. Or is it that you are afraid to finish what you started?"

"What I started?" she threw at him.

"What was I supposed to do?" he said, feigning the innocence of a sleepy panther.

"Kept your lips to yourself for starters," she said, feeling the heated hum of his kiss as she stared out at the blur of paddocks.

8

———

What had made her angry? He had not been overly zealous with his kiss. He had held back his passion. While he was renowned for his strength, his ruthlessness, and his complete command of the world around him, he never sought to possess a woman. And yet, she has as good as accused him of taking her against her will.

Most of the women he met, and all the ones he bedded, were compliant, subservient, irritatingly meek. Something about Kate's indignation excited him—but also incited caution, Gianni mused.

But there was no mistaking the longing beneath the kiss. The desire. The chemistry too strong to fight. He had just been having a little fun. Why had she denied him? It was unheard of, the challenge she posed excited him.

"It's so dammed humid Kate said, wiping her forehead as they bounced along the unpaved, rattling country road. She stuck her head out the window as they sped past a clutch of rural farmhouses. Winding potted dirt roads led to homes patched with worn wooden planks and corrugated rusting iron.

Gianni lifted his eyes from the road momentarily and glanced toward her. Her pale face was flushed, luminous, pure. He felt his heart tug. It was extraordinary how beautiful she was. God, he'd like to kiss her again. He already knew she tasted delicious.

Just don't call her *babe*. He'd made that mistake and it wouldn't be one he'd be repeating. Nope, she was no *babe*. She was a goddess, he thought, an angel on a mission, united with him, bringing gifts to the poor.

He glanced in the rearview mirror, lingering for a moment at his reflection. He on the other hand was the devil incarnate. Wasn't that what the women he had bedded told him when, tiring of their infatuation with his body and his wealth, he severed them from his life so ruthlessly?

But this woman, he thought with a certainty that startled him, she was too hot not to hang on to. She was white-hot fire, he thought as he glanced over at her. Kate's long, flame of hair, tumbled provocatively over full breasts which jiggled like Christmas puddings as they sped down the badly main-tained rural roads of the Far North.

Gianni dredged illicit thoughts of Kate's body from his mind and fixed his gaze firmly on the road.

He did a good job faking happiness. Why now, as he looked at her did it feel so real? Gianni had felt immediately drawn to her. And something about her told him that, despite his cynicism, she could thaw his heart.

He liked what she had to give. The spirit, the strength, the life force that radiated from her like a bright light. Despite the enigma she presented, he wanted to believe in her, like children wanted to believe in Christmas.

Clenching the steering wheel, he dislodged the thought firmly. What he needed was a freezing cold shower. Even a goddess couldn't work miracles.

The only things that brought Gianni any comfort was acquiring businesses, mergers and takeovers and the accelerated earnings that inevitably followed—things he could control and get rid of without any remorse. Anything else left him cold. Which suited him just fine. Money brought power, freedom and choices, and right now he chose to be free—forever and *always*.

Perfecto.

"It's true, Italians are crazy drivers," Kate said, startling him from his thoughts. "Slow down. Look at the dust you're throwing up. Everyone's houses will be full of it."

Gianni glanced in his rear mirror again, noticing for the first time the billowing clouds trailing across the sky in their wake. He took his foot off the accelerator, slowing as they drove past signs which read, *Slow. Dust.*

Slow.

He didn't do anything slowly. Gianni lived his life at breakneck speed. His body bristled with irritation. No one told him what to do and now with the fury of a Formula One driver this damned woman had come crashing into his life delivering orders. Worse, he was powerless to disobey. This would not end well.

He slowed to a crawl as they approached a tiny settlement of houses poised at the edge of the peninsula. Kate waved to a little boy, bare-chested and clad in tatty shorts, who ran from the side of the road. A chorus of cries, accompanied by a wave of giggling and a sea of flailing arms and skinny brown legs, as children emerged from their homes, followed the Land Rover as it rattled down the lumpy dirt road.

Children with huge glistening dark eyes ran alongside them as they approached the marae. Kate turned toward Gianni, beaming with happiness. His heart skipped. It was not the smile of a show pony but brimming with a rare authenticity that cantered through his soul.

His heart was pounding so heavily he was certain she could hear it thrashing against the cavity of his chest. What the hell was wrong with him?

Get a grip. Fast.

Gianni had cultivated his reputation as a stone-hearted bastard for a reason. Staying rigid kept his demons at bay. But his censor floated out the open window as his gaze trawled the length of her candy-striped stockings, travelled along the little satin bows at the top of her thighs, then thrust toward the rise of her satin clad breasts.

Gianni felt his appetite for recklessness flame. It was Christmas and this year Santa's helper would be his present.

9

———

Kate opened the door for Zac and he froze, every sense aquiver. He instantly took in the whole scene: a bright summer day, acres of pasture, a dozen horses, a clutch of kids, and two dogs. A light breeze rustled Manuka leaves, wafting scents of hay and horses across the rural farmland.

Doggie heaven.

In half a second Zac flew out the door, a black blur zipping toward the pasture. He raced at full gallop one way and reversed, paws tearing up the dust in a skidding turn, then accelerated to warp speed in the opposite direction. His mouth agape, the corners pulled back in a canine grin, his tongue lolling out one side.

"For a little fella with three legs that dog of yours is a fireball," Gianni said, as he watched him zip ahead of children laughing as they ran after him. "Aren't you worried how the horses will react," he asked as Zac blasted into the maze of animals without hesitation.

"He can hold his own," she said, inwardly sighing with relief as the horses didn't shy.

In a flicker, the kids, dogs and horses all joined Zac who was consumed with the joy of play, as he initiated a free-for-all game of follow the leader.

"Pretty impressive," Gianni said, grinning as Zac darted from horse to person, to dog, to pony, to person, and back to horse in an outstanding display of speed, athleticism, and pure exuberance. The children squealed with delight and ran after Zac as he did figure eights.

His gaze met hers as he turned toward her and she flushed.

"Come on," she said, turning away. Gianni and the other adults joined her as she ran toward Zac and the children, whooping and running. Even some observing Tui's got caught up in the act, swooping over the melee.

The moment was captivating, gleeful, unexpected, and short-lived, Kate thought with disappointment as the horses scattered and the dogs lie down, panting and cooling their bellies in the grass.

Gianni and Kate caught their breath and laughed. She felt the tension and fatigue fall from her shoulders. The kids circled them giggling. And then it dawned on her, for the first time in forever she felt completely exuberant.

10

The rest of the day had a lightness and ease that Kate hadn't felt for a long time. Zac had given a compact demonstration of the power of fun and play. The children had carried their presents away, filled with excited anticipation of opening their gifts on Christmas day. Maybe everything would be okay, Kate mused as she lifted Zac into the passenger seat and sat beside him.

"What kind of dog is that, anyway?" Gianni said.

"He's not a dog. He's a person," Kate said. "He's Zac. But if you must know he's part pug, part manic depressive." Kate said, frowning as she caught Zac's melancholic gaze. "Zac, could you please stop looking at me like that?"

Zac sighed and leaned closer to Gianni, gazing longingly at his lap.

"He likes to drive," Kate said to Gianni.

Zac looked up at Gianni with love. Traitor, she thought.

"Could you do me a favour?" Kate said. "Could you let him sit in your lap? Just for a minute."

That will tease out what sort of guy you really are she thought. "He likes to stick his head out the car window. He loves the way the wind blows up his nose, only thing is it makes him fart."

Gianni looked down at Zac. "Whatever he needs, *mia cara.*"

Kate stared at him. Was he for real? "I'm not joking. He really farts. Smelly, stinky ones."

"I grew up on an island which belched sulphurous gas every day. Nothing phases me."

"You lived on a volcano?" she whispered. Her lips pressed tightly together.

"*Si*, Stromboli. Do you know it?"

Kate shook her head. No, and she didn't want to either. Her hands curled into fists.

"It's a volcanic island," he began, oblivious to the terror drumming through her body. "It is one of the few volcanoes in the world that is *always* active. There's an explosion every few minutes, sometimes it lasts for hours. This has been going on without interruptions for the last 1300 years. It is very dangerous. Sometimes it blows up and lots of stones go firing up and plummeting down. It makes a big hole in the earth and burns everything around."

Kate grimaced. "It sounds horrid."

"It was all I knew. It wasn't without its rewards."

"Rewards? You've got to be joking."

"People loved to visit my island. When I was young I was very popular with the foreigners who liked to flirt with danger," his eyes glinted mischievously.

"I bet," she said.

"I think It was because I was so cute."

Cute wasn't the word that sent fire blazing down her spine.

"If it erupts, it kills you," Gianni said.

Kate bit back a confession. She wanted to tell him she knew all about death by a volcano but she was afraid all the tears she kept bottled inside would explode in boulder-weight grief.

"Why did you stay?"

"I felt safer there than on the mainland. At least I only had to deal with nature. Not the mafia-wars, men and their greed. There was none of it there. It was safe. We were a small tight community."

Community, she mused. Like her beloved bees.

"We called the volcano, *iddu* In Italian this means 'him'. Because he is like a friend, a person, someone loyal who is always there."

"I would rather eat fire than make friends with a volcano," Kate said, angrily.

Gianni turned to her, a quizzical line rippling across his brows. Kate knew what he wanted. He wanted to explore what made her so red-hot furious. But she said nothing. How could she trust him with her feelings? Her memories? Her pain?

She couldn't even trust herself.

"As kids, we used to draw *iddu*. Some kids drew him with

a heart over his crater. Others as a guardian watching over the school and the children playing in the courtyard."

"Weren't you terrified?" Her fists softened, she splayed her fingers on her thighs.

"No. it was like thunder. Beautiful. Like you," he said, turning to her.

"Flattery doesn't suit you," she said, unable to suppress the faint smile that fluttered to her lips. But then she remembered. Keep your distance. If Gianni saw all of you, the you that is hidden beneath your clothes, beauty is not the word that would ooze from his lips. Scarred. Disfigured. Damaged.

"I hate thunder," she scowled. "And I hate volcanoes."

"Maybe, *mia cara,*" he said, softly. "Maybe you would love this volcano."

"Not a chance."

He shrugged. "Perhaps," he said, smiling, "In time you will go there."

"You've got no idea."

"Try me," he challenged.

She wrapped her arms around her chest and turned to look out the window.

"Everything shakes, but the normal explosions, the ones that happen all the time, we don't hear them because *iddu* is so far away. Like you are now. Where have you gone?"

"I'm trying to picture how living on a volcano shapes a person. The constant dread. The never-ending fear that tomorrow you may never wake. The everlasting pain that loss brings."

"I didn't see it that way. In many ways, I had an idyllic existence, especially for a child. We were surrounded by water. We would row in our boats. Fish. There were no cars or motorbikes. We had donkeys and skateboards for transport. We lived in simple white plaster houses. We had no iPad, no

Internet, no stereos. We just played in nature. My childhood on Stromboli reminds me of New Zealand. It was an isolated and incredibly beautiful existence."

"Why did you leave? What made you come here?"

He stiffened, his mood briefly darkening."I came to visit Leonardo. I liked it here. I stayed."

"Oh," she said, not wanting to pry." Everyone had secrets. He could keep his, just like she would keep hers. "I ran away from home when I was four," Kate said. "I can't remember why. I regret it now." She felt a wave of longing wash through her belly. What she would give to turn back time.

"That's where we are different. I don't regret anything," Gianni said. "The past is the past and the future is what one creates."

"You make it sound easy."

"It's a choice," Gianni said. "So what will yours be?"

"I wasn't aware I needed to make one," Kate said.

"About me."

"You?"

His eyes, that intriguing shade of amber that sometimes looked like gold, glittered as he pulled the Range Rover to the side of the road and stopped the engine. Zac regarded them with smiling eyes, then turned, and padded to the back seat as Gianni leant toward her.

She missed hugs. She missed being held. She missed cuddles. Her soul ached with need. She closed her eyes, holding back tears of longing.

Her heart hammered, then stopped as his arms wrapped around her. She felt an iron wall of terror slam between them. I can do this, she silently affirmed, willing the wall to yield. I can let myself be hugged.

His hug was honest, caring, real, she registered as she folded into his chest. She sighed with relief. His hug held no demand. His hug was not a grope. His hug asked nothing of her. Just that she allowed herself to be loved.

A wave of guilt surged through her. God, what was she thinking? "I have things to do," Kate said, tearing herself away. She wasn't ready. Perhaps she never would be, she mused, ignoring the conflicting desire swimming through her body.

"Perhaps I can help?" His tone held no hint of her rejection.

What was it he had said, 'I'm an acquirer. I always get what I want.' Was it possible he wanted her? All of her? Despite the fact she was a cot-case. But why?

Well, maybe she should join the acquisition business too. She had to move the beehives again. The fact was an extra pair of hands, particularly, attached to muscular arms as powerful as Gianni's would shortcut the effort. She couldn't allow herself to be loved, but she could allow herself to acquire his help.

"I enjoyed today," he said. "I'd like to get to know you better."

"I'd like that," she said, ignoring the fear that pounded through her.

Spending more time together couldn't hurt, could it?

11

"Wow, this is quite a set-up." Gianni said, surveying the three dozen beehives nestled below Manuka trees misted with bunches of white sweetly scented flowers. "When you said you had work to do, I don't know, I imagined something else."

"What? Like manicuring my nails?" Kate said.

"No, no," he said, thrusting his hands out, palms facing

toward her. "I've never met a beekeeper before. You continue to surprise me."

"My dad discovered the curative properties of bees before anyone else caught on. Honey's hot business now. But when he first started it was his passion project."

"And now it's yours?"

Kate flinched and locked her gaze on a swarm of bees buzzing around the base of the three stacked boxes that held the frames where the bees stored their honey.

"I'm looking after things for him," she said, quietly, putting the lid firmly on painful memories she didn't want aired.

"Our ancestors were amongst the first to settle in New Zealand from Britain and unlike many English settlers, they built very close relationships with Māori. They taught his father about the curative power of plants and bees and dad followed on."

"Your dad was a visionary," Gianni said.

Kate felt her heart go all gooey like honey spread on hot toast. I know what you're doing, she thought silently. You're trying to win me over. You're just saying that so I fall for you. Well, I'm not buying it. *I can't.*

"The Manuka plant was known for its healing properties in early New Zealand, with Māori using most elements of the plant for medicinal purposes," Kate said, deftly steering the conversation toward the safer passion—her bees. "James Cook even made his own home-brewed Manuka and Rimu beer to help his crew ward off scurvy."

"I didn't know that. That's interesting," Gianni said.

Encouraged, Kate continued. "Dad began researching the antibacterial and healing properties of Manuka honey, and he travelled to China and discovered what they were doing there with burns victims—and the seed was sown for huge commercial success. There are so many more markets now." She didn't mention the lack of money which prevented the realisation of their big dreams.

"Bee Healthy," Gianni said, looking at the label on one of the first jars of ointment her father had made. "I like it. It's simple and spells out the benefits."

Kate felt her face heat. "Thanks. That was my idea. My father was toying with calling the business *Espra*, but I mean, what's that? It's not even a real word."

"Exactly. Some brands are too clever. Like your Kiwifruit brand. *Zespri*. It's confusing. Why didn't they just call it was it was and trademark that? But Bee Healthy is great. I'm no expert but I do know that Manuka honey has become a global must-have. You've got a brilliant mind and a brilliant idea."

Was his compliment sincere? Should she trust him? Dr Joe's mindset strategy buzzed through her mind. She decided to try a drizzle of raw vulnerability.

"I made the mistake of introducing my Dad to a guy I was dating," she said. "He went behind our backs and tried to steal the global distribution rights. Fighting him in the courts sucked up a lot of energy—and money."

Gianni's fingers tightened around the jar. "I hate cheats. That was plain wrong."

Kate wanted to hug him. He got it. He got it straight away. So many people had told her that was just business. That her father had been naive. Instead, she just shrugged. A hug might lead to a kiss, which might lead to sex under the Manuka trees, which might lead to. . . Stop it! She affirmed silently. Your mind is carrying you away with the birds—and the bees.

"I can't shake the feeling," she said, trying to dislodge the desire heating her body, "that the past is a predictor of the future. The experience changed me. And let's face it, humanity is only becoming worse."

"So that's why you don't trust me?" Gianni asked.

Kate shrugged.

"You think the same thing will happen? Is that why you keep your secrets?"

"Everyone has secrets," she said. "Secrets aren't for sharing. That's why they're called secrets."

Gianni ran a hand over his designer-stubbled jaw, considering her words. "You have shown me your home, now let me show you mine. I don't take many people, certainly not a woman into my intimate space. But you're different. You are special."

She cast her eyes toward the faint pink blush tinging the clear blue sky. Did he really mean that? "I don't know," she said, trying to repel her curiosity. She'd heard it said once that a person's home was a reflection of self. What exactly was Gianni's self? For that matter, what was hers?

"It's getting late," she said. *Late.* The word struck her. Was it too late for her to change who she was and become who she wanted to be?

"The sunsets are incredible," he said. "It's the best time to see the property. "Besides you seem stressed," he said, pressing lightly on her tensed-up shoulders. "Relax," he laughed. "What's the worse that could happen?"

She compressed her lips so no words would escape.

"You might just have a good time."

She bit on her full lower lip and sucked a deep breath. That was exactly what she was afraid of.

12

———

T*ūrangawaewae*, Kate read as they approached a large wooden plaque, elaborately carved with Maori symbols.

"You live here?' Kate asked, disbelievingly, as the Land Rover crested the top of the hill and drove through the towering security gates. She had heard of *Tūrangawaewae*, everyone had. It was known to locals as the hermit Kingdom, where one of the world's most reclusive bachelors resided.

You could read about his vast estate, but you could never visit his sacred sanctuary.

Gianni nodded. His face impassive. Modest. Heat fanned through her. The fact that his chest wasn't all puffed out with self-importance only made her respect him more.

She inhaled a giant gulp of fragrant air as she savoured the postcard-perfect sea views. Dusk was falling. The setting sun washing the sky with pinks and lavenders, reflected in the still ocean, framed by islands, below.

"This must be the most beautiful place on earth," she exclaimed. Stretching endlessly before her lay a spectacular coastal retreat unfolding within the natural paradise of the Bay of Islands.

"I've died and gone to heaven," she murmured. Her heart felt like it was going to burst out of her chest.

"I'm glad you like it," Gianni said.

"Like it? I love it!" she blurted before she could censor herself. What her Dad would have given to see this, she thought sadly.

Her gaze swept along the pristine beaches, registering the sparkling marine playground and luxury super-yacht, acres upon acres of rolling farmland and native bush alive with birdsong.

She noted the four secluded luxury guesthouses peppered through the expensive plantings of native bush and meticulously cultivated lawn. Kate thought of her own haphazard garden which, even if she had more time and more money, would never match this luxurious pristine paradise. The whole place screamed billionaire.

She glanced at Gianni. He didn't look the least bit enamoured with his money or his luxury estate. In fact just the opposite. He was looking at her like she was the most valuable thing in his life.

A shrill voice rang through her ears. "If you're not careful Kate, you'll fall under his spell."

Kate tore her gaze away from Gianni and explored the extraordinary estate. The property sat on a peninsula at the northern mouth of New Zealand's stunning Bay Of Islands. Gently sloping acres overlooked Rangihoua Bay, framed by farmland, lush native bush and regenerated wetlands. To the left a vineyard had been planted, adding to the natural beauty and abundance.

"How much land do you have?" she asked, registering the army of groundsmen trimming flax, raking leaves, and mowing vast expanses of lawn. Despite the activity designed to maintain cultivated perfection, the feeling was of sublime serenity.

"A thousand or so acres," Gianni answered. "It wasn't always like this. Originally it was a run-down sheep station. I've worked with locals to realise *Tūrangawaewae's* potential by rejuvenating and evolving the land while maintaining a sincere nod to its heritage, people and culture."

"You own all of this?" she said, unable to comprehend how one man could own such a large slice of paradise. She mentally computed how many hives she could position around the estate.

"I prefer to think of myself as a long-term guardian. Locals refer to it as our *tūrangawaewae* (place to stand) – love, respect, sustain and care. These are the values most important to me."

Kate's eyes stung because she could see that Gianni was telling the truth. As the Land Rover continued its journey toward the main residence, she found herself thinking, how different her life would be if she let him care for her. Her heart flooded with heat.

It wasn't just his money. Gianni valued the things she did.

Nature. The land. Beauty. *Love*. Oh, boy, she was in trouble. She had left the safety of her home and ventured into his domain.

A warm breeze lifted a tendril of hair and swept it across his face. She wanted to catch the trade winds in her own sails. She wanted to allow herself to explore, dream and discover how life might be lived if she allowed herself to be loved.

What she didn't know was, after all this time of deprivation and emotional numbing whether she could be loved, even if she wanted to be.

13

———

What had she been thinking? Why had she accepted his invitation from this lion of a man to step into his lair? While he was neither fierce nor dangerous he was clearly a skilled seducer, she mused as she regarded her surroundings.

Gianni's bedroom reminded her of the stories she had heard of sultans harems. Embroidered silk hangings billowed from the ceilings, and heavy Flemish tapestries covered the walls. Crystal bottles filled with exotic scents stood upon ornate chests. His intimate surroundings were so different from the exterior she had traversed upon arrival. Gianni was as fascinating as he was unpredictable. A frisson of sensual awareness scuttled up her spine as he drew closer to her.

Oh God, he's going to kiss me. Again.

Kate could see it in that stern set to his beautiful lips. That raging fire in his gaze. Worse, she could feel it in the way she simply melted. Everything inside her turned soft and ran sweet like honey on toast.

It was as though she was meant to bump into him at Christmas. As though he was her surprise present. He was something, or someone, sent from above to save her from her sadness. She thought she'd never wanted anything more in all her life than the press of that sensual mouth of his against hers. Again. And again. And again.

Just one more kiss, she lied to herself, almost wistfully, as she looked up at him. Who was she kidding? He was an addiction she would never be able to kick.

"Don't kiss me," she whispered, too quick, too raspy, and too revealing. "I don't want you to kiss me again."

Gianni's uncompromising mouth was so close. Too close. The look in his eyes was enough to raze whole cities. There was no disguising the way it made her tremble.

She didn't try. What was the point? Her desire was emblazoned through her mind, body and soul.

Gianni drew closer still, his arms moving around her to hold her there in imitation of a lover's embrace. Or perhaps it was no imitation, after all. Perhaps she was more than a sympathy score. More than an empathetic conquest. More than a "Sorry, I wasn't thinking" seduction.

"Let me see that beautiful face," Gianni held Kate's chin in his fingers and turned it towards the candlelight.

Her face. She could let him see her face. But not the rest of her. Not those scars, she told herself. Just a kiss. One kiss.

I can stop before we go too far. But her assuring words faded as she surrendered to his touch with a mix of intoxication and adrenaline.

She should leave. Now. She should. . .

And then he claimed her with his mouth. His probing tongue rendered her powerless. Her lips parted like a flower opening for the strident force of the proboscis of a bee. It seemed inevitable. Fated. Destined.

"I want to taste your sweet nectar," Gianni said, as though reading her thoughts. He pushed her shoulder gently so that she fell back on his bed. He leaned over her and kissed her cheek, and then trailed his kisses down her neck. His touch was far more tender than she had expected or dared pray for. Far softer than the furnace of desire she saw in his eyes.

"I want to make sweet love to you."

Kate groaned as his lips peppered kisses around her neck. She lifted her gaze to the window as he kissed her ears. The moon was full and ripe with promise. Endings and beginnings, she thought to herself.

I can do this. I can let him love all of me.

She felt nervous, but tried her best to conceal her fear. Smiling coyly she held her gaze steady and looked directly into his eyes as they searched her face.

I can do this. She affirmed again. *I can let him love all of me.*

Her gaze followed him as he slid his hand along the rise of her breasts, then down along her stomach, pausing beneath the rim of her jeans.

I can do this. I can let him love all of me.

Her belly trembled. She hoped her fear didn't show.

I can do this. I can let him love all of me.

The button of her jeans surrendered easily, loosening away, revealing a glimmer of flesh. Gianni's eyes were pinned to her. So far so good. He try to unzip her but the fly snagged. She held her breath as he tugged at the zipper while still maintaining a look of sensuous control.

Gianni smiled and rose to her, as he released her zipper with the deftness of Italy's most skilled lover. Kate writhed upon the sheets, surprised at how his fingers brushing against her bare skin pleasured her.

And then she remembered.

Remembered the ugly scar that wove a jagged line from her belly button to her womanhood and down her thighs.

Remembered the raw, raised reminder of the love that had died. The sacrifice they had made. The survivor's guilt she couldn't shake.

"I can't," she rasped." She braced her hands against his chest. She couldn't have said if she was pushing him away or, far more worrying, simply holding him there.

And then she ran before she destroyed them both. "Take me home."

14

"I've met someone." Gianni squeezed his powerful frame into the tiny pink upholstered chair in Issy's counselling room.

"But that's great," Issy said.

"It's complicated."

"Complicated? You mean like Gianni Romano complicated?"

Gianni grimaced. "Worse."

"Wow. That is complicated. Is that why you're here?"

"You're a counsellor."

"Yip. And you're my husband's best friend. You didn't need to book an appointment because you've finally found someone you like. We could have talked over dinner."

"I didn't want you to think I was using you. You know. Abusing our relationship. Disrespecting you professionally. I need to talk things through."

"What kind of things?"

Gianni shrugged. "You know—stuff."

"I'm honoured that you would want to open up to me. Honestly. I am. But it's kinda awkward. Ethically…"

"I wouldn't be here if I didn't need some—" he paused, suddenly conscious that he hadn't stopped fidgeting with his hands since he had arrived. "The thing is," he mumbled, " I need some—"

"Help?" Issy offered.

"*Si*, that." He studied his lap. Gianni had never been to a therapist but he knew he was putting Issy in a dilemma. Issy knew he had an MBA in self-reliance. He was counting on the fact that if he was asking for help she would know it had to be something important. Important enough for his powerful athletic frame to be filling the tiny pink upholstered chair in her counselling room. Important enough for him to be sitting next to a box of tissues risking making a damned fool of himself.

"She's beautiful," he began, his voice trailing off. "Her fiery auburn hair shines like the Sicilian sun," he began as his gaze followed the arching lilt of the flowering flame tree outside the window.

He saw the reaction in her clear green eyes before she spoke.

"Flaming red hair? Waist-length?"

"*Si*. You know her?"

Issy gulped and studied her lap. "Complicated, you said. What makes you say that?"

"I kissed her."

"That's it?"

He shrugged. "She did a runner. Women never do that. Not to me. Why didn't she stick around?"

Was that relief he saw in Issy's face as her shoulder's loosened?

"You've come to see me because for the first time in your life a woman you want doesn't want you back? Oh, Gianni. You remind me of Max when we first met. Every other woman he had ever met was needy, demanding attention and continuously distracting him from his work. Or tortured and conniving, in search of a fortune or wanting to party, party, party. But I wasn't like that, and it drove him wild. I was a woman he couldn't control."

"I shouldn't have come."

"Has it crossed your mind that you want her because she doesn't want you? I'm asking as your friend, Gianni I can't be your counsellor. But I can counsel you…as someone who cares about you," she paused. "I had a client once. Let's call her Mandy. A terrible tragedy happened. So terrible Mandy could barely talk about it. She was diagnosed with survivor's guilt."

"Survivor's guilt?"

"People who have survived when others they loved died, often experience crippling guilt. The symptoms come under the umbrella of Post Traumatic Stress Disorder. Survivors often experience flashbacks of the traumatic event, obsessive thoughts about the tragedy, spikes of irritability and anger, fear and confusion and feelings of helplessness and disconnection."

"*Fanculo*," he said, raking his finger through his hair. The poor woman. What did this…this *Mandy* do?"

"She went to counselling to get professional help and learn some tips for overcoming self-blame and quilt. She started learning it wasn't her fault. That she should and could get on with her life."

"Can others learn these tips to help? People who care about *Mandy*."

"They can….the thing is…how do I put this….if you want to help someone like Mandy you need to be pretty committed. It takes a lot for people with survivor's guilt to trust, to open their hearts, to learn to love again. Often they feel so guilty and so disconnected that even if you want to love them—all of them, scars and all—they don't know how to be loved. They won't let themselves love. They won't expose themselves to loss."

"Are you saying I'm not up to the job?"

"No, Gianni. I'm not. It's just. . . "

"Say it."

"You're a commitment phobic," she said, softly.

Yes, he thought with surprising relief. And look where that's got me. 35, single, and without a family.

"Can you help me with that?"

15

"I owe you an explanation," Kate said, driving Gianni toward the blazing red flowers of the pōhutukawa. Owe wasn't right word, but the idea to open up had been planted by Issy during their last therapy session when she had shared how she had fled Gianni's bed.

Gianni felt like saying, "dammed right, you do", but he remained mutely silent. A week had passed and she had ignored him. And now she had called to make amends.

Gianni sat back in the passenger seat, balancing Zac on

his lap, as he regarded the intelligent, passionate woman sitting beside him. Instead of seeing her as a self-absorbed, know-it-all, he now saw a compassionate woman, so damaged from the unfathomable trauma she had endured, that he wanted to dedicate his life to easing her suffering.

"Today marks 12 months since my family died."

"I'm so sorry," he put his hand over hers and rested it there.

Despite her grief she smiled weakly as though moved by the kindness of his touch and genuineness of his words. He didn't ask what had happened. He already knew and when she was ready, if she was ready, Kate would trust him with her memories.

"Is that why you push people away? Because you're afraid you won't survive if you love again? Because you're afraid of someone you care about dying?"

Her gaze caught his, and in that moment he knew she understood that the someone he spoke about was him.

"My father was so strong, like you," she whispered. "Such a fighter, such a tower of strength."

She pulled the ute to a stop, opened the door and thrust her feet upon the soil. "I scattered their ashes under the sacred pōhutukawa tree over there," she said, gesturing to the blazing red giant standing in a prominent place surrounded by hives of bees.

"It's a beautiful place to rest," he said.

She smiled weakly. "Māori legends tell of the young warrior, Tawhaki and his attempt to find help in heaven to avenge his father's death. He subsequently fell to earth and the crimson flowers are said to represent his blood."

"Blood and beauty. Life and death," Gianni said. "Endings and beginnings."

She looked at him, confused awareness glazing her eyes.

"I ache and cry every day," she said, as she lowered herself and sat beneath the wooden cross planted amongst the roots. "I'm trying to be strong. I'm trying really hard to show my dad that I'm not giving up on the life he wanted for me—kids, a husband, a family."

He felt his heart kick. *A family.* Every electron in his body did an exultant dance, the air charged with sensuality, as his thoughts turned erotic. Why did his body want her naked in the dirt, to take a chance on love and start a family? He censured himself. She was grieving. She was in pain. She was baring her soul. And all he could do was think about impregnating her.

Insensitive brute. You should be ashamed.

"This was one of my father's favourite places," Kate said, unaware of his battle for control. "I scattered his ashes here. I like to believe that mum and my sister's ashes floated over here too," she shrugged. "You know….because I can feel them around me, like they're looking down from heaven . . . like the bees, sometimes, I just get the feeling…you'll think this is silly…but I get the feeling they're my family when they buzz around me."

Gianni nearly smiled, as a swarm of bees approached. "It's a sign. "

"Do you believe that?"

"*Si*, I believe in omens," he said, as a bee settled on his shirt. "I'm Italian. We believe in such things. I know that since ancient times, bees. . . especially honey bees, were seen to bring messages from the Divine. They are associated with the soul and to bring the blessing of fertility."

Kate blushed. "Look," she wiped a tear from her eyes, "That one's Kristie and that's Dad," she said as another bee settled on his chest."and they like you."

"I am glad. I do not wish to be stung," he laughed.

"I'm grateful that they aren't suffering anymore. I convince myself that Dad and mum and Kristie are holding each other tight in heaven and sometimes when I need them they come back as bees. Flying around happy and free. Together, having fun, sitting in flowers and playing. I like that thought the most. That they're happy and very much alive. That they're always with me. Does that sound crazy?"

"No, *mia cara*, that does not sound crazy. The Greek philosopher Pythagoras believed that the souls of the wise and ingenious passed into the bodies of bees. In many traditions, bees were associated with other world messages, the soul, and heaven. The Celts and Saxons believed bees were winged messengers between worlds. Egyptians thought the bee represented *ka*, the soul."

"How come you know so much about bees?"

"I know your love of them, so I made it my business to love them too."

"You did that? *For me*?"

He leant over and lifted a wisp of hair from her face, then wiped the tears staining her cheek with tender softness. "According to Egyptian mythology, when the god Ra cried," he said softly, "his tears turned into bees upon touching the ground, to deliver messages to man."

"What kind of messages?" Kate asked.

"That you are loved," he said.

She flinched and looked away. "I loved them so much and I am trying my best to make them proud. They gave me the best life possible full of love, support and so many opportunities. I promised my dad that I would live."

"And what of love?" he asked, taking her hand. "Did you promise him that you would love?"

"Yes," she whispered.

And then she fell back upon the grass, whispering the words he had waited so long to hear.

"Love all of me."

16

____

F eel the fear and make love anyway. Isn't that what her therapist, had told Kate? 'Go hard. Don't overthink it'.

Hard, Kate had decided was the act of stripping bare, and making love under her favourite tree in bright sunlight, with nowhere to run, nowhere to go, nowhere to hide the scars that rippled across her thighs.

Hard was facing the silent terror that Gianni would not be able to love her. *Not all of her.* Not without closing his eyes to blank out his disgust. And even then, if he could endure her disfigurement, *hard* was knowing she would be nothing more to him than a sympathy screw.

Stop overthinking, she told herself as Gianni lowered his powerful frame and knelt beside her. Anxiety wormed through her gut. She focused on Gianni's hands. His fingers were long and sensuous. *Too sensuous.*

I can do this, she affirmed silently. *I can let him love all of me.*

Gianni drew her hand to his chest. She felt a hard mound where his heart was, but it was not that which her fingers touched. He guided her hand inside his shirt pocket. Her fingers cupped around a soft pouch full of what seemed to be stones. She looked at him, confusion addling her brain.

He patted the soil beneath the giant pōhutukawa tree. "Release them," he said.

She withdrew the small ink-coloured silk satchel and spilt the contents onto the ground.

Jewels!

She looked at him, not knowing what to make of the gesture.

"Choose the one that makes your heart glad."

"I couldn't," she said, bewitched by the precious gems.

"I want you to be happy, *mia cara*. Don't deny me this pleasure," he commanded her.

Kate sat up, ignoring the worry that the reason he wasn't rushing to make love to her was because he didn't find her attractive. She willed her racing mind to focus on the iridescent display of brightly coloured gems. Instinctively she reached for a slightly heart-shaped honey coloured diamond, tied with a gold satin bow. She held it up so it caught the sunlight. She was rewarded with a display of brilliance as prisms of light ebbed and shimmered through the summer air.

"You chose well. This is the stone of virtue. Pure like the

infinite sky. It has many powers," Gianni said, taking it from her and gently pressing it between her breasts.

They locked eyes and Kate looked away first because she was imagining herself entwined beneath his beautiful body. That muscular chest, those taut shoulders, that...*that smile.*

"It is the gem of gems. Just like you, *mia cara.* Overflowing with outstanding purity. A combination of characteristics blending into one very exceptional treasure."

Gianni's tone was soothing and seductive, yet comforting at the same time. How was it possible that in such a short time they had come to mean so much to each other? Was he more than she deserved? Would he be taken from her if she allowed him to love all of her?

"It shields the wearer from pain and sadness and is an antidote against heartbreak."

Kate shivered as he spoke. If only it truly possessed that magic. She gazed down to where the jewel still lay pressed upon her chest. If only she were so flawless.

The gift was beyond anything she had ever been given, and now she wanted to give him a gift too. An inexpensive gift, but far more priceless. She wanted to give Gianni her heart.

She could do this. She could let him love all of her. Couldn't she?

"It's magnificent," Kate said, summoning her courage. "Truly remarkable," she said. Her fingers tightening around he diamond as she placed her palm to it. She appreciated that he was not rushing to make love to her. His patience and consideration only endeared him to her more. It was as though he knew she was terrified of his judgement and wanted her to lead.

"But not as remarkable as you," Kate added, as she placed

the diamond carefully on the raised root of the ancient tree towering over them protectively.

She fell back on the warm earth and gazed up into the canopy as Gianni lay beside her.

Please, please, love all of me.

Gianni curved toward her, his hands wrapped around her waist and he held her tight as he pulled Kate against his chest. "I'm glad my gift delights you, *mia cara.* You deserve to be happy. We both do." He leant over her and kissed her cheek, and then trailed kisses down her neck.

His touch was far more tender than she had expected or dared pray for. Her body trembled with longing and anticipation.

He began to slowly unbutton her shirt. He kissed her breasts, lingering over her hardened nipples. Her heart gave an exultant leap.

Kate sucked a deep breath as he unzipped her jeans, the folds of denim loosened away, revealing a glimmer of flesh. She gasped and held her breath. Her heart seized. How would he react when he saw her scars?

His eyes were pinned to her. She held her breath as he tugged at her jeans. She writhed against the warm earth trying to maintain an air of sensuous confidence.

He nuzzled closer to her face, then whispered into her ear. "Kiss me kiss me, and then kiss me again, with your richest, most succulent kiss; then adore me with another kiss."

Poetry. He was whispering poetry. Her heart fluttered. Can it be? The richest, most powerful man she had ever met, a man whose reputation inspired fear as much as adoration, was whispering love sonnets.

Her breath faltered at sweet and unexpected words.

"Ten more kisses, sent just for your pleasure," he murmured.

His lips were soft, sensuous, desirous. And she was pleasantly surprised that instinctively, like a bee to his honey, she yearned to sample his nectar.

Her body quivered. She was surprised how his fingers brushing against her bare skin, rather than terrifying her, pleasured her.

He took his time undressing her as though savouring a fine wine. He scented her again, lifting his face to hers, trailing his nose down Kate's neck, lingering over the rise and fall of her breasts.

Gianni sucked a deep gust of air into his lungs. Then exhaled slowly as he moved along her stomach. Kate suppressed a giggle because his breath tickled. Above her the native Tui's called to each other in exquisite bird song and fantails playfully ducked and dived. The drone of bees filled the air scented with Manuka.

For the first time since the tragedy, she felt free. Whether it was all the therapy sessions or a spontaneous madness that had gripped her she didn't know. All she knew was that she want to touch him, pleasure him, love him, but he pushed her hand back gently as she reached for him.

"You need do nothing," he said. "It is my role to bring you pleasure."

She didn't know how to take his command. Wasn't she supposed to be the one pleasuring him? It was all she had ever known. To sacrifice her own needs to others. But she sensed from the look of delight that sparkled in his eyes that Gianni was getting more pleasure from her than any other woman he had ever bedded.

She did his bidding and lay back and prayed that he would not be fast. Having allowed herself to be so vulnerable she wanted to savour every moment. She wanted this to last. Last longer than she dared admit.

Her body ached and yearned for release as he continued his travels down her body. She sensed he did not wish it to be over. He took his time familiarising himself with every rise and fall of her curves, learning the terrain of her, as though he was reading a map of her soul.

He pulled her jeans from her. Kate braced herself for his disgust. There was no longer any hiding of the horror that marked her. No longer any seeking refuge in the sound of the birds and the bees and the warm summer breeze. Kate turn slightly on her side, anxious to shift the sense of foreboding that flooded her.

Rather than wince and pull back with repulsion Gianni lowered his face to her scars. His lips hovered and lingered over the raised rivulets of her scars. Slowly, sensitively, seductively he kissed the white and leathering patchwork of skin that had been taken from her butt. And in that miraculous moment she felt the trauma lift.

He kissed her wounds as though the scars were not there. He kissed her as though he did not care about her marks. He kissed her as though what he felt in this moment would linger for many years.

"I have seen almost all the beautiful things that God created. I have enjoyed almost all the pleasures a man can experience. But never has a woman aroused me so," he murmured as he kissed her again and again.

Kate wanted to weep. Instead, she closed her eyes and silently prayed. Thank you, dear Lord. Thank you for answering my prayers.

He trailed his tongue down her legs. Kate's fingers gripped the soft grass as his tongue found her most sacred place.

"Stay still," he murmured as her body trembled. She

heard in his tone that he was taking pleasure from this different form of control.

Her back arched in rivets of delight. A river of desire flowed with every lick and touch of his warm, soft lips against her sensitive skin. Kate closed her eyes and surrendered—mind, body and soul. She was barely conscious as she felt him straddle her. She was dreaming of him.

Was it a guilty pleasure to be enjoying this? Before Kate could deny herself Gianni entered her with slow, rhythmic movements that probed her deepest longings.

They made love and then when she was sure he was sated, she touched him again in the sacred spot, below his sac, which she had discovered gave him so much pleasure. He rose again like the virile stallion she had found him to be. Aroused, they made love again. He rode her at a gallop, then slowed to a canter, a trot, a peaceful ride along the stream of delight she never wanted to end.

17

As Kate got dressed Gianni's gaze lingered over the diamond pendant he had gifted her. "We've all got scars," Gianni said. "Some are deep, and some are hidden. They define you, but they don't have to ruin you."

She had given herself to him and now he knew that he needed to share something of his own hurt.

"My father," he began, tripping over his words. "Wasn't like your father," he said clumsily. Why was this so hard? Because you don't do emotion, he muttered. You don't talk emotion. He didn't or hadn't spoken of his father in years and now he felt compelled to share.

"You were lucky," he said. "Your father loved you more than the birds and the bees. It wasn't like that for me."

That was enough, he told himself, censoring himself as a swarm of bees encircled him. It wasn't the right time and he had said too much already. It suddenly occurred to him that repairing his scars, which were so deep that no relationship he started ever endured, required a Herculean effort. One he was bent on making. With a little help from his friends he mused as he regarded the winged omens.

He wanted to believe, as the ancient Greeks had, that these tiny striped creatures possessed curative properties. He wanted to possess the blind faith Kate did that bees held a powerful ability to transform lives.

He only hoped that these were friendly bees, he mused as they settled on the bare nape of his neck. Fearlessly they gaily travelled down his powerful chest, marching a beeline toward his heart that for so long he had thought devoid of feeling.

Bee Healthy, the name Kate's father had given to his fledging honey empire flew to his mind. Perhaps the painful memories that stung them both could be turned into something good.

18

K ate would never know what gave her the strength to share her story as he stood there and stared back at her, sharing his pain and capturing her own in those dark unfathomable eyes.

"It was supposed to be a happy moment. The trip of a life-time. A Christmas cruise around the most beautiful parts of New Zealand. The cruise was winding up. The last excursion was to the volcano on White Island. My parents were apprehensive but I talked them into it." Her voice cracked. "We were told it was safe."

Gianni remained silent. A tower of strength, instinctively knowing that nothing he could say would ease Kate's pain.

"Instead my entire family died beneath a river of lava and a storm of volcanic rocks when it erupted. I'll be honest. I wanted to die too. I remember the nurse saying to me, 'Are you glad to be alive?' No, I told her. 'I wish I'd died.'"

"I'm glad they're being sued," Kate began. Anger made her voice shake as she began to tell Gianni the secret she had kept for too long.

Kate felt disconnected from her body. It was as if she was talking about someone else. I am, she told herself fiercely. The *Kate Miller I was died that day and she's never coming back.*

"I was choppered out of the remote island barely alive and wasn't expected to survive. I spent over six months in hospital. I had over 230 operations. I suffered full-thickness burns to 35% of my body."

She wanted him to know her. All of her. She had told herself that she didn't care what he thought. She now knew that was a lie. She wanted to lay herself bare. Scarred, scared and scorchingly vulnerable.

"They sent me to successive shrinks, none of them made a difference, no one could get through to me. Until I met Issy. She was different. Against overwhelming odds, I defied every expectation and rebuilt my life. Last year, I achieved a goal I'd been working towards since the early days of my recovery. *Keeping my dad's dream alive.* Saving the business he founded from dying became my mission. I won award after award after award for our honey. It felt too easy. The guilt never left me, but I convinced myself, it was all for my dad.

Like he was there with me, watching over me and cheer-leading my success. Does that sound crazy?"

"Crazy beautiful," Gianni said. "You are a beautiful warrior who would not stop fighting no matter what."

His words tasted like honey. Strengthened by his admiration she continued on."White Island was a gruelling experience that taught me over and over again that when we get our mindset right, we truly can achieve anything. My career mindset was mind-blowing. But I couldn't say the same about my personal life."

"You threw yourself into work to numb your pain," he said. "I understand that."

He was too kind, too caring, too understanding. But her scars ran too deep for him to breach the fortified walls that protected Kate from loving anyone again. Kate wanted what she didn't deserve to have. She wanted his love. But she didn't crack. She didn't open. She didn't soften her resolve never to love again.

They had made love, but it wasn't love. Not like that. *It was a thing. A fling. A something,* she told herself. She didn't know what it was. Only, that she had done as Issy challenged. She had felt the fear and she had exposed herself. She had bared her scars and she had had sex. And he hadn't rejected her. That felt good. She couldn't deny that. In fact, it felt better than good. *It felt wonderful.*

She narrowed in on her anger, shifting her focus from her treacherous feelings for him. "The reason those cruise ships took people to White Island that day was pure profit. Greed. Heartless hunger for the dollar. *Whakaari* had shown signs of increasing volatility for weeks before the eruption and they didn't alert anyone. They just kept taking everyone's money and sending men, women and children to their graves."

She paused, aware she had left her body. Disassociation,

Issy called it. She forced herself to say the words she still believed. "It was my fault. It was my idea. The cruise company didn't force my family there. I did. I killed my family."

"No," Gianni said, softly. "No."

Little words which meant so much. But Kate's pain was too much to bear. Her eyes swam with tears and she looked away. "I was keeping my fingers crossed that somehow dad and mum and my sister would survive. I thought perhaps they had found somewhere to shelter. A cave, the water, something," she sobbed.

Gianni's strong, protective arm wrapped around her. Kate allowed herself to nestle into him.

"And now to hear that they're taking trips there again—" she took in great gulps of air as he rocked her gently, caressing the trauma from her body.

"It just seems," she searched his face. "I don't know. I feel conflicted. If we closed everything off after a disaster there'd be nothing left. Life would not go on, but—" she shrugged.

Wasn't that what she had been doing? Closing herself off? Now that she had opened to Gianni, would it be a mistake to erect the walls around her heart again?

"What you've endured is unimaginable," Gianni said. "I can't even begin to fathom your pain. I wish there was something I could do."

"To be honest," she began, "Just listening to me," she fiddled with the edge of her sleeve. "I dunno," she shrugged. "Not like a therapist. Like a—" she paused. *Like a husband.* "It's helping," she looked away.

"It's been the strangest, saddest time. I threw myself into my work. I tried to numb the memories with business. Memories of how heartless many people were. How people were only motivated by self-interest. Like the journalist who approached me as I sat in a cafe during the excruciating wait for developments. 'Are you family?' he asked. 'Did you lose someone, or escape the island?'"

"Who does that?" Gianni said, sharing her anger and despair.

"A 70-strong media pack clogged the waterside, looking for grieving family members who had sought refuge in motels that had stationed security guards in their forecourts. They didn't really care what I felt, what *we* felt. They just wanted to make their new reports more fleshy. So I told them, 'No I didn't lose anyone. I'm a reporter.' And I retreated into myself."

"Self-preservation," Gianni said. " I understand that."

Kate shook her head. "I lied. It's not something I take pride in."

"Have you always been so hard on yourself?"

She paused. *No, not always. Just since I killed my family.*

"Many locals said they'd held quiet fears about the possibility of an eruption for decades. They said it was only a matter of time until it blew during one of the increasingly frequent tours."

"None of this should have happened. But nature doesn't play fair," Gianni said. "You can't blame yourself. Nature is unpredictable. She can't be taken for granted."

"I should have known," Kate said. "I knew something was wrong. I pushed them to go."

"You didn't know. How could you?"

Kate shrugged. "Locals knew. Some Māori viewed White Island's eruption as a sign of the volcano's dissent and protest. That 'she'—as locals describe her—was sick of increasing numbers of tourists and boats traipsing across her bones. And she blew to show humans her power. I talked to local residents. One woman told me that she had never been to the island. She believed that *Whakaari* was a living being, one of her ancestors. She had been telling people that the island should not be disturbed. That too many people were capitalising on *Whakaari's* good nature. But no one listened. So the volcano blew."

"The truth is that modern tourism is out of step with nature," Gianni said.

Kate felt a soothing warm heat flood through her. Here was a man, looking at her as though she was the only person in the world, who understood. Who knew how she felt.

Who would be her undoing.

She wanted to throw herself into his arms. She wanted to feel his protective arms around her. She wanted to feel safe. She wanted to feel his mouth on hers again. His taste. His touch. His heat.

But the truth was she didn't deserve happiness. She had other responsibilities now, far bigger ones. Her quest to make her father proud was far more important to think about than her own dizzy pleasure, or this far too handsome man who had consumed far too much of her thoughts already.

"My family, and others paid with their lives," she said, pushing away from him. "I can never forgive that. But tourism is not only the lifeblood of Whakatāne, it is an economic necessity. It is located in one of the country's most socio-economically deprived regions. There are few other big money-earners in the region. I see my bee empire as providing an alternative economic rescue," Kate said.

"While I admire your altruism," Gianni said, "the wider community is not your concern. You need to think about you. Me. *Us.*"

"Don't you see," Kate flung at him. 'That's the problem with the world. *Me! Me! Me!* We've become a world obsessed with our own concerns. Bees don't think like this. Bees are all about community."

Gianni's face changed. His arrogant expression dimmed, and something far more considering gleamed gold there in the depths of his dark gaze. "I'm sorry," he said softly.

She felt how dangerous it would be to believe that those two words, wrapped in a melodic voice that sent goosebumps prickling all over her, held the mark of sincerity. Kate wrapped her arms around her chest to keep herself from shivering in reaction.

"You are still grieving," Gianni said. "I know that. I respect the fact that you want to make a difference. That you don't want people to go back to the old ways of earning money and risking the chance that more innocent people perish."

"Locals are nervous that the notoriety may stain their town forever. I need to do something. I need the death of my parents to mean something," Kate said.

"You're driven," he said. "I admire that. You want to turn one of our largest tourism disasters, major for your small town and New Zealand's tourism industry as a whole into a success story," Gianni said. "Perhaps I may be of help. If you would allow me."

His voice was dark and hot against her skin. "How could you help me?"

"I have lived under the shadow of volcanoes all my life. I understand them. I respect them. I love them."

Love. Why did he look at her that way when he spoke? The word lilted through her like a song, lyrical and perfect.

"Ordinarily, I am not a gambling man. I am renowned globally for my decisive, business acumen and vision. I seldom take risks. But with you, *mia cara,* with you it's different. Together, I know we can build something great from this tragedy."

"We?" Kate said.

"We," he said, emphatically.

"Sell me, Bee Healthy."

19

Kate's hair was a tousled flame. Gianni longed to run his hands through it all over again. He could see traces of the tears she'd cried earlier on her cheeks, but she was not weeping now. If anything, she looked ready to explode.

Gianni waited for the moment she would blow in protest, and fury. He was still learning about her volatile moods. She blew hot and icy cold. Usually at a second's notice. But this time Kate just stood in stoic refusal.

She stared back at him, an eruption raging inside her. "Rich men are well-known for their disarming nature," Kate said, coolly. "Befriend and betray. That's the tactic isn't it, borrowed from the CIA?" She raked her hands through her flaming red hair.

"What sort of monster are you? I was sharing my heart. And all you could think about was how to take over my business. I can't believe I fell for it. *You.* I'm so stupid. I trusted you, Gianni. I thought you truly cared about me. I mean, what are the odds—a girl who almost died in a volcano meets a boy who lived on one? But now I see what I really mean to you. I'm just another score. Another acquisition. Another conquest. Or rather my business is. I thought it hurt when my family died. No, hurt is not the right word. Nothing paints it like it is. Just like nothing captures how I feel right now. You will not, can not, shall not, buy your way into my life. Bee Healthy is for sale only over my dead and buried body. I'm leaving."

Gianni strode ahead of her as she marched toward her ute. He pressed his weight against the door as if determined to keep her there merely by holding the vehicle in place.

"There's no way in hell I'm letting you out of my sight." He couldn't let Kate leave. He had to make her stay. He had to make her understand that his need to possess what was hers was driven by his own guilty secret.

But how could he explain? This was Kate Miller. The only surviving relative of the Miller family. Everyone else burned to death. Her mother and her sister's remains were still on the island. Unease permeated his soul. He could have prevented the accident. But where to begin. She would never forgive him. How could he explain that he thought the one solution was to redeem himself the only way he knew how.

With his fortune.

"At least you're up front," she said, bitterly. "Not like my last excuse of a boyfriend who went behind my back. Why on earth would I sell my business to you? Other than some useless mythology you've rote churned, you don't know anything about bees."

"I don't need to. Someone else can run Bee Healthy. You could start over. Move away. Begin a new life."

"A new life?" she threw at him. "I don't want a new life. How dare you think you can take the only thing that gives me a reason to live? I've been a fool. I thought you loved me. *All of me*. But nope, you just loved my bees. Or rather, the money you hope to make from them," Kate corrected.

Her words stung. The red-headed siren he'd come to love was rejecting his offer. By default, she was rejecting him. But rather than concede defeat, her fierce refusal only made Gianni more determined.

"Step back from the ute," Kate hissed at him "And get the hell out of my life."

"Not going to happen," Gianni said.

Her defiance ignited a spark. A dangerous thought burned in his loins, blazing through him in a siren of red more fiery than a Sicilian sunset. Would he come to regret this decision. Would mixing business with pleasure be the bedrock for a lifelong love? Or would it all explode like an angry volcano?

"What do you *want*?" she hurled at him. "I told you Bee Healthy is not for sale. My parents' memory is not for sale. *I'm not for sale*. Why can't you get that?" Her beautiful lips pressed together in a grim, determined line. "Leave me alone."

"I can't do that."

"Can't or won't?" She stood there as strong and unmoving in her volcanic volatility and started back at him.

"I'm sorry," he said.

"Sorry? You're not in the least bit sorry."

And then the energy between them shifted, as though she had suddenly discovered a palpable lie.

"What did you say your father did again?"

20

"My father was a dishonest man," Gianni said, without pausing to consider the ramifications. "He was not a man I could ever love. He turned our home on Stromboli into a gambling house. But he was not as clever as the other inhabitants. He lost a lot of money. And I mean, a *lot of money.* My father said to my mother, 'let's leave.' But she did not want to leave her beloved Stromboli. She did not want to flee in disgrace. So she said to my father, 'you leave.'"

"I'm sorry," Kate said. Her voice oozed compassion but her eyes were wary.

Gianni shook his head, more as if he was shaking off a memory that had lodged in his mind than tossing off her empathy. "Don't be. I'm not," he said, with a harshness that surprised him even as he spoke.

"I'm asking about your father. I'm asking you to help me understand. Because if he's who I think he is—" Kate's body had the stillness of a wild animal whose every sense was alert, suspicious and untrusting.

"You already know the truth. In your heart. But that's not what you want to hear, is it? Because you're afraid."

Kate stiffened as if he'd slapped her.

"For better or worse? Which is it to be?"

"You're talking in riddles," Kate threw at him.

"*Will you love all of me* if I tell you the truth?"

"I detest lies," she said, quietly urging him on.

"My father agreed to leave on one condition. 'You keep the children,' he threw at my mother. 'As long as you never ask me for child support.' *His children. Me!* My mother was strong like you. She loved us. She agreed. So he left. I never saw him again."

"He abandoned you," a fierce frown creased Kate's brow.

Gianni wasn't sure he could continue but her empathy fortified his resolve. "You want to know the truth. Here is the truth. He is a crook. He steals, robs and destroys everything and everyone he touches. He made it his mission to take money from men who were gambling. He got mixed up with a bad crowd in Sicily. The mafia financed his big ideas and supported his gambling houses. Now they are all over the world. . . .these casinos," he spat. "It's disgusting. The harm they create. The food they take out of the mouths of families. The victims."

"So your father chose a life of crime over you?"

"I prefer to think my mother saved me from a destructive man," Gianni replied. "On Stromboli, you couldn't run away. You didn't have a place to escape. Not as a child. I stayed. And I stayed with the threat of the volcano. Because if you live with the volcano and don't exploit him he won't hurt you. Unlike my father."

Kate felt his pain. Felt his abandonment. Felt his grief as if it were her own. Despite the difference in their circumstances, he too had known loss. Not the loss of his family through death. But a loss far worse. The loss of a father who failed to provide for him and then acted as though his son was dead.

"Then what happened?" she asked.

"He came back." Without warning, anger exploded in Gianni's chest. "He came back with a big story about how Stromboli could be a huge cultural capital. Musicians, artists —gamblers. High-rolling ones. I didn't want any part of it," he felt the rage he had stored for so many year ebb from him as he spoke. "You're the first woman I've shared this with he," he confided.

Kate's eyes glistened, as though she could see that Gianni was telling the truth.

"So I left. I left to find my own fortune. I knew it was only a moment in time before my father became disinterested in us again. And then my hope, my dream, was that I could create a sustainable future for my mother, and my sister so that they could live freely."

"So you left one remote island for another. New Zealand?"

"Yes, an island with no memories. Or so I thought. Until I met you," Gianni paused, gathering the strength to share his horrific discovery.

"I didn't learn of my father's involvement with the consortium who owned the volcano and ran the tours that killed your family until yesterday."

"You knew how they had died before I even told you. Why didn't you tell me?"

"I was afraid of losing you. I had already fallen for you. When I found what my father had done, the things he did to conceal the dangers—" his voice trembled as he spoke. "I knew if you found out I wouldn't stand a chance. But now I see my mistake. I'm so sorry. Please forgive me. If you can find it in your heart to to trust me again I will devote my life to ensuring you have no regrets."

Kate raked her fingers through her hair.

"You asked me to love all of you—scars and all. I guess, Kate, I'm asking you to love all of me. Even the blight on my character having the disfigured DNA of a man I'm ashamed to call my father." He pulled in a ragged breath. "Do you want to love me?"

"You make it sound easy. Like you just *decide* to love someone," she whispered.

"Isn't it time we stopped dragging all our baggage around? Don't you yearn for a fresh start?" he said. "It was wrong of me not to tell you. And it was arrogant of me to assume I could just takeover Bee Healthy. I wanted to help. But now I see it's not something I want to do on my own. I want to partner with you in the fullest sense of the word. I want to help you realise your father's vision to help people recover from life-threatening burns."

Kate's auburn brows curved into a frown. Not the frown of an angry woman, but a woman perplexed by the man dangling temptation in front of her.

"With my wealth and your brilliant mind we could change people's lives. I've spent my life trying to escape my painful memories. I want to live my life creating new memories. Happy memories."

Gianni got down on one bended knee. "Happy memories filled with a wife, children—if you'll have me. *All of me.*"

"You're proposing?" Her eyes were bright, gleaming with emotion, reflecting a love he felt she wanted but fought to deny.

"I don't know. This is all so fast."

"Come home with me," he said, sensing the turmoil creating rivets in her heart.

"To the volcano?" she said, keeping her eyes on three bees buzzing around them.

Gianni took her hands in his and drew her to his chest. "If you can love me there, you can love me anywhere. I want you to understand who I am. I want you to meet my family. I want you to love all of me. Then you can give me your answer."

21

———

"I decided to live on the island in 2011," Gianni's sister Frida told Kate as they sat beneath the night sky on the terrace overlooking Stromboli's rocky shoreline.

"Actually it happened by chance. I had planned to go to Mongolia but in the end I didn't go." Frida rolled her dark eyes. "Boy problems. I came to Stromboli to heal my heart. I came for a month. Left. Came back. Left. In the end I said, 'I want to live on the island.'"

"Don't you feel isolated?" Kate asked, gazing out at the Tyrrhenian Sea stretching endlessly before them. In the distance she could barely trace the northern coast of Sicily's mainland.

"*Si*. It's a quiet island in winter there are 300 people. Strong winds and grey skies drive people away. I like that there are not many people."

"Me too," Kate said.

"But in the summer it swells and it is horrible and we can barely move. Thousands of tourists call onto the island arriving in boats. It's so crowded."

"Like Kerikeri during the tourist season," Kate said. "Coaches and camper vans crammed with tourists block streets. And cruise ships taller than the 144 islands dotted in the ocean clog the sea. It's bittersweet. On one hand, the locals need the money, on the other, we all crave peace," She gestured to *iddu*. "Aren't you afraid of the volcano?"

"Him?" Frida said, gesturing to the plume of smoke. "He is my passion. I trained to become a vulcanologist so I could understand him. He's been letting off steam for decades. A bit like my brother," she laughed. "*Iddu* is constantly active with minor eruptions all day. He had a major tantrum last year, sending tourists fleeing into the sea. But it was nothing. So no, I am not afraid. I respect him. This island, for better or worse is home. Yes, I am far away from the world, but it is home. It has an extraordinary energy and *iddu* is important to volcanology. He is the lighthouse of the Mediterranean, named for his steady towering glow. He is our protector."

Kate's mind drifted to Gianni "He's magical," Kate murmured. "I love it here. I didn't expect that."

"And my brother?" Frida asked "Will you let him love you? Will you let yourself love him in return?"

Kate lifted her fingers to the heart-shaped honey coloured

diamond Gianni had gifted her, now hanging from a fine gold chain around her neck.

Feel the fear and get married anyway. Isn't that what Issy would tell Kate? 'Follow your heart. Don't overthink it'.

Her gaze drifted down to the black-sand beaches gleaming under the fiery sunset.

"I will," Kate said, and the moment she uttered those two little words she felt her sorrow dissolve.

"To heal is to cherish the wound," Frida said, rising to her feet. "The full moon will arrive soon. It will heal your heart." She reached into the camel-coloured leather bag slung from her shoulders. "Try this," Frida said passing Kate a notebook and pen. "Write it out, purge, and release. Journal your desires and your fears. Focus on healing the old wounds and shedding whatever you don't want to carry into the new year. Ask your soul what matters most and attend to that."

"You sound like Issy."

"Who's that?"

"My therapist."

Frida laughed. "I should do. When our father abandoned us I spent a small fortune on therapy."

Kate watched as Frida disappeared toward the village and then began to write. She poured her heart onto the page. She wrote out her fears, her guilt, her shame, all the blame she had carried for too long. She allowed herself to feel, really feel, her deepest desires and longings.

"What matters most to you, my soul?" Kate said out loud as the moon, rich and ripe with promise rose above the horizon. Her hand flew across the page as if guided by an angelic force.

'My heartfelt desire is to love and be loved and through that to send more love into the world.'

. . .

SHE STARED at the page for a very long time. One word demanded to be written. She resisted until she could not anymore and at last she wrote, in large, confident, capital letters.

'BABIES.'

Her heart kicked and then fell into a peaceful lullaby. Kate felt joy for the first time in months. She lifted the pages from the notebook and then gently tore the paper into tiny confetti-like shreds. She rose to her feet. She cupped her hands and blew them kisses as she released them to the sea.

"May I join you?" Gianni said. And when he smiled it was like daybreak.

Her heart danced an exultant jig. She drew his hands to her mouth and kissed them. "I love you," she whispered. "I love you more than the moon and the stars. I love you more than I feared volcanos. I love you with all my heart."

Gianni took her in his arms and kissed her deep and long. Strong fingers raked through her hair, scattering the pins she'd used to secure it into a bun on the top of her head. As her auburn locks tumbled freely Kate felt as if something in her had mended. She had the strangest feeling that he was the key that fitted her locks and she was the lock that fitted his keys.

"Kate Miller, have you reached a decision. Will you marry me?" he drew back from her and bent on one knee before her.

"Yes," she cried. She placed her hands on his chest as he rose to his feet, feeling the rhythmic unison of their heartbeats.

The first stars trembled into life in the indigo sky, illuminated by the fireworks glowing from the volcano.

"Gianni Romano, I would love to be your wife. Your love has given me back my life."

He reached into his pocket, took her hand and placed a dazzling emerald-cut diamond ring on her finger. "You have made my wish come true. The only thing I wanted for Christmas was you."

In the distance, the sound of children's laughter filled the air.

"I just wanted you for my own. More than you could ever know," she laughed, remembering Mariah Carey's song lyrics.

He was the man she had dreamed she would spend her life loving. He was the man she had dreamed she would have children with. He was the man she had vowed she would marry.

And now her dreams were coming true.

22

Tiny little fairy lights wound over the white plaster walls lining the streets lighting the way toward the little church which looked out over the sea.

In the distance *iddu* spewed fire, illuminating the sky in a natural show of fireworks.

All eyes turn toward Kate, as she entered the church with Zac padding proudly beside her. The contrast between her flame-coloured hair, and porcelain skin hidden beneath a veil of lace shrouded her in serene mystery, created a stir of hushed approvals.

Kate nodded and smiled at Jacqui and Issy who beamed at her in unison.

Gianni stood at the altar and turned his head and smiled mesmerised by the powerful magnetic force pouring from his heart toward the woman he loved. Beside him Leonardo Bressolini held the rings.

Kate wore a dress of beautiful Italian antique lace, around her neck was the diamond he had first gifted her with his love, and a very simple cross that Gianni's mother had given to her. A symbol of her eternal blessing for the marriage. Gianni glanced toward his mother. Her eyes filled with tears as she clasped hands with Gianni's sister, nodding her approval at the woman who was about to become her daughter.

As much as Gianni wanted the wedding to be over, so he could take his beauty to his bed as his lawful married wife, he didn't want this beautiful moment that he once thought would never arrive to be over.

She wore a garland of white mountain flowers in her hair, complementing her natural beauty. She looked a picture of radiant, flawless beauty.

Kate walked slowly toward Gianni, the giant emeralds glittering in a sea of diamonds in the engagement ring she wore on her finger, complementing the intense green of her eyes.

Their gaze locked on each other, a magnetic magical spell wove around them like ribbons lacing their souls together drawing them closer and closer. The church was full but in that moment Gianni saw no one but her.

The candlelight flickered, sending out the sultry scent of beeswax. Kate had insisted she create her own candles. The soft flames lilted toward her, imbuing her in an intoxicating scent of honey.

"May the Lord be with you and may God Almighty bless you in the name of the father, the Son and the Holy Spirit," the priest began.

Iddu roared from his belly like a happy dragon of good fortune.

"Do you take this man as your lawful husband?" The priest asked Kate.

Kate looked at Gianni with those big infinite eyes. "Will you love all of me? In sickness and in health, for better and for worse?"

"I will," he said, softly.

She turned to the priest. "I do."

"Do you take this woman as your lawful wedded wife?" The priest asked.

"Will you love all of me, in sickness and in health, for better and for worse?" Gianni asked, his eyes searching Kate's face.

"I will," Kate said, solemnly.

"I do," Gianni said, turning to the priest.

Gianni heard his mother silently weeping as they slipped the wedding rings on each others fingers.

"I now pronounce you wife and husband. You may kiss the groom," the priest said turning to Kate and winking.

Gianni lifted the soft white antique lace veil from her face. Kate tilted her head up toward him her eyes searching his. He bent his head toward her parted lips and then sought oblivion, staking his commitment, his vow, and his claim to love her forever.

The soft ballad the violinists played was suddenly replaced by the heavenly song of young choir boys. Their voices filled the church almost drowning out the roaring exclamations given by the volcano blowing his approval in the distance.

Tears of joy flowed from Kate's eyes. At last they were unchained from their painful pasts. They were free to love, and they knew they would live happily now and forever after.

* * * *

THE END

LOVE ALL of Me is now available as an audiobook for your listening enjoyment. Check out a free sample or grab your copy from your favourite online retailer or library.

AUTHOR'S NOTE

This story was inspired by the tragic events of December 2019 when the volcano on *Whakaari*, commonly known as White Island, in New Zealand erupted. At the time of writing, the eruption took the lives of 16 people and injured 30, most were critically hurt with life-threatening burns.

I read about a young man (aged only nineteen) who not only was severely burned but awoke from his induced coma to learn that his entire family had died.

I wondered, what would it be like to be a survivor? What if you were wracked with survivor's guilt? What if your scars weren't just on the outside but buried deep within? What if you felt you had no right to live, let alone love again? What and who would it take to heal such traumatic scars?

The story was also inspired by my father, G.W. Gaisford who discovered a miraculous way to help heal deep burns using an emulsion created in part from honey. I'm proud to say that my father cured so many people who would otherwise have been left with disfiguring scars.

I wondered, what if my heroine wanted to follow in her father's footsteps and as a result founded a honey empire.

Where I live, in the Bay of Islands, the Manuka flower attracts many bees and a great many successful companies have been founded here. It astounds me how clever, and vital to life, bees are.

I wrote my first draft in the notes section of my iPhone as news of the fatal volcanic eruption on White Island unfolded.

P.S. I hope you enjoy meeting Issy Riley again, The art therapist you met in *Married by Christmas* (later renamed The Italian Billionaire's Christmas Bride.) Read on for a BONUS excerpt.

Leonardo Ermenegildo Bressolini, from my short story *Forever and Always*, set in the Bay of Islands, New Zealand, made a brief appearance too

If you'd like to learn more about these characters, gain inside tips into the writing process, or be the first to know when a new book is released, subscribe to my newsletter here: http://eepurl.com/ghM501

Please email me and I'll be in touch personally—I promise…mollie@molliemathews.com.

WOULD YOU LIKE TO JOIN MOLLIE'S READERS GROUP ON FACEBOOK? It's a private group that all of my readers are welcome to join. There is nothing that makes my heart sing than to connect with you all and talk books and writing, and I so appreciate the encouragement and support you give me.

Join Mollie's Readers Group here:
https://www.facebook.com/groups/323525616931811

AND FINALLY...

Thank you for purchasing and reading my books. You are more than my livelihood—you let me live my passion. Without your love of romance and belief in the power of love, this book would never have been born. I really hope you loved *this story* as much as I enjoyed writing it. Here's to an extra-ordinary level of love and happiness in all our lives.

With love,

THANK YOU

Thank you for reading *Love All of Me.* I hope you loved it. If you did…

1. Help other people find this book by writing a review
2. Signup for my new releases email to find out about the next book as soon as I release it, sign up here http://eepurl.com/ghM501
3. Email me at mollie@molliemathews.com with a copy of your honest review and let me know if you'd love to join my dream team and of advance readers
4. Follow me on BookBub, https://www.bookbub.com/authors/mollie-mathews
5. Stay in touch on Facebook, https://www.facebook.com/molliemathewsnz
6. Follow me on Twitter - https://twitter.com/Molliemathewsnz

7. Be inspired on Pinterest - https://nz.pinterest.com/molliemathews and Instagram - https://www.instagram.com/molliemathewsauthor
8. Follow my blog - https://www.molliemathews.com/category/blog/
9. Watch me read from my books on Youtube: MolliemathewsYouTube

Keep reading for sneak peeks into other passion-filled stories including *The Italian Billionaire's Christmas Bride* and *Claimed by The Sheikh*

EXCERPT: THE ITALIAN BILLIONAIRE'S CHRISTMAS BRIDE

THE ITALIAN BILLIONAIRE'S CHRISTMAS BRIDE

Mollie Mathews

Blue Orchid Publishing

THE ITALIAN BILLIONAIRE'S CHRISTMAS BRIDE

Mollie Mathews

Blue Orchid Publishing

PRAISE FOR THE ITALIAN BILLIONAIRE'S CHRISTMAS BRIDE

"A good read that takes you away to a tropical island to experience the steamy heat of two people determined to stay single in case they get hurt again. Max, a sexy, jaded Italian multi-billionaire meets up with Issy, a playful children's art therapist who has recently found out her fiancé was having an affair. Although I was initially skeptical as I usually go for historical romances, I'm glad I trusted my friend's recommendation because this book was delightfully compelling. The emotional vulnerabilities and character quirks combined with the sexual tension kept the pages turning. A frisky novel to curl up on the couch with or take away on your next trip."

~ Pauline Roberts

"This was a fun read I really enjoyed. It's perfect for a lazy weekend. This is the first book I have read by this author but it won't be last. I can't wait to be more."

~ Poppy

"Beautifully written. The author's vivid and descriptive writing style pulled me into a world I never wanted to leave. I loved the connection of art between two very different people and the healing it brought them both. A Very beautiful story!"

~ Hugh Harrison

"I joined Max to make the slow journey from betrayed broken-hearted individuals to the trusting and loving couple they become. Molly Mathew's writing transports you to places she is describing where you can kick back and relax for a while as this endearing story unfolds. Her characters soon become visible through her careful picture-building. Readers will like the Kiwi vernacular Issy invoices every now and then, and I think readers will enjoy getting to know the strong characters and the beautiful islands we're visiting. The author also tucks in some great life advice for everyone telling in the telling of this charming story. I hope you enjoy this book, too. I did."

~ Alfie Rues

"I loved, loved, loved this book. An instantly gripping, compelling and fun read. Escapism at its best. I couldn't put the book down and read it in one night. With exotic back-drops like Italy and Fiji and passionate characters, it made the perfect holiday read. Can kindness thaw a cold-heart? That's the question Mollie Mathews poses in her book about second chances and learning to love again.

Issy is a funny, compassionate art therapist who wants to escape Christmas after her jerk of a fiancé cheated on her. Even though she only works with troubled children she agrees to take on a last minute client for her friend and business partner. What she doesn't know is her client is hunky fashion house CEO Massimilliano Balforni. Sparks fly and it's an attraction Max vows to deny. He doesn't want Issy and her colored pencils from bringing the wounds of his childhood to the light.

Mollie Mathews skillfully creates a gripping dynamic between Issy and Max that sensually blends their animosity with undeniable attraction making the tension soar. I definitely recommend this book."

~ Lauri

One word frees us
of all the weight
and pain of life:
That word is love
~ Sophocles

1

'*Che cavolo!* No! No! No! This will not do. Only an anorexic model could wear something that resembles a straw,' thundered Massimilliano Balforni, CEO of Emporio Balforni, Milan's most prestigious fashion house. His coal black brows knitted in a fierce line as he looked with disdain at the scatter of sketches the young designer splayed on Max's 15th Century walnut desk.

His protégé began to protest but one piercing look from the maestro forced his lips shut. His body stiffened as if frozen to the floor, reminded that his employer's wrath was more dangerous than black ice.

'Alexandria Gorbetz is a real woman, the world's richest woman, and someone like me that demands perfection.'

Max's mouth curved in a controlled smile. Was that fear he detected in the young man's face as Max pierced him with his dark gaze? He had every reason to be afraid. Enemies and friends alike knew Max had destroyed promising careers for lesser transgressions. Infinitesimal precision, extraordinary control, unrivalled beauty—Max suffered nothing less.

Pressing his fingertips to the smooth, cool parchment, he

paused momentarily as a childhood memory stirred in his consciousness. He sucked in a breath and swept his hands brusquely across the page. He was no longer the lonely child who furtively sketched movie stars in beautiful clothes and dreamed of a Hollywood life.

What was once an escape was now a thriving commercial enterprise with insatiable demands. Max flourished his gold fountain pen across the page, adding a sweep of curves to the hips and breasts of the bespoke wedding gown his fashion house had been commissioned to design.

Now at the helm of his multi-billion dollar empire Max was no longer a hands-on designer, but nothing went out the door without his final veto. Some called him a control freak and this he took not as a criticism but as the highest compliment.

He waited to feel the rush of joy he used to feel when drawing as a child. He stopped to await the all-consuming love that arose from knowing that no one possessed his raw talent and genius. He paused to feel the pride that came years later from knowing he designed dresses perfectly, to satisfy only one client on her most important day. There was nothing.

It shouldn't have surprised him. He had long ago accepted that he was unable to feel the joy that other people did. He'd turned off that part of himself years ago and had vowed never again to succumb to vulnerability. In its place, carefully groomed aloofness and instilling fear in others were traits he prized and relentlessly cultivated.

As his protégé braced for the consequences Max forced his thoughts back to the commission. While he felt nothing in his heart, what he did experience as he looked at the drawing of the wedding dress executed to his design was a coolly detached appreciation that satisfied the perfectionist in him.

The lines and structure now conformed absolutely to his definition of ideal. The controlled steel gray pallet reflected his personality and every detailed aspect had been meticulously executed as he had commanded. No randomness or chaos anywhere.

Having witnessed his parents' brutal marriage and subsequent divorce, Max had no misguided notions of happily-ever-after, nor any desire to marry.

Perfection in relationships was simply unattainable. But the knowledge that he was at the helm of an empire that created exquisite, extraordinarily elegant gowns admired by the world's most elite, at the same time preserving a historic tradition, filled him with a degree of pride.

But as for the rest of his life—the personal, emotional side—he felt nothing. And that suited him perfectly.

Max's long supple fingers drummed an impatient rhythm on the armrest of his chair. '*Allora?*' Well? People react to fear, not love, he reminded himself as he kept his voice soft, but somehow containing all the might of the towering spires of the Duomo looming beyond his window.

A slither of fear crept into the young designer's hushed apology. 'I should have thought more about the woman beneath the dress.'

'Thinking is not enough,' Max commanded, his voice a dark, stark thing in the quiet of his office. 'You must apply.' Taking the drawings in both hands he tore the pages down the middle. 'Begin again, and this time bring me excellence.'

Ignoring the tiny pin like tremors piercing his chest Max pushed back from the desk and rose to his feet as the young man retrieved the torn fragments and scuttled quickly toward the door. Striding across the room Max willed his racing heart to cede to his control.

2

'Calm yourself, please Maxie,' Sophia Balforni said, sweeping into his office she cast the young man a sympathetic look as their paths crossed. 'Have you thought about what I suggested?' she asked, gesturing to the art therapy brochure peeking from beneath a pile of contracts.

'I am surrounded by amateurs and now you want me to play like a child, *mia sorella.* I have never heard something so ridiculous.'

'You're my brother. The best brother in the world, but do you know what's holding you back? You're afraid of losing control. You're afraid that without all of this', she said, sweeping her hand around the room, 'you're worthless.'

'But all of this means nothing if you're dead. And none of this means anything without someone to share your heart and soul. I hope one day you're able to realise that you're wonderful for who you are, not just for what you've accomplished. But most of all I hope you're able to experience the unconditional love and support of someone who loves you for you.'

Max was neither given to excessive emotion nor impetuousness but his mood wrestled with his need for control. He threw open the shuttered windows of his office and inhaled the frigid Milano air with shallow, measured breaths.

He ran his hand over his broad chest, fingering momentarily the fine scar snaking across his heart. His mind had the endurance and stamina of one thousand oxen but two months ago his body had betrayed him.

His gaze swept down the Piazza then flew up the spires of the Duomo, dusted with snow and bejewelled in dazzling pre-Christmas lights as the cacophony of Vespas buzzed like irritated wasps through the open window.

Although he had always hated Christmas, he loved tradition and he loved the supreme elegance that the Milanese never failed to deliver, but it pained him to concede that never had his beloved city been so irritating. In fact, everything, and everyone was irritating. Even his designs bored him. He knew better than most that he must continually innovate or die. Grudgingly he accepted his sister was right. He needed to get away.

'I admit it's a little unconventional,' Sophia said, taking an assortment of pills and vitamins from a gold embossed pillbox. She poured a glass of mineral water into a crystal tumbler, she passed the pills and water to Max.

'Unconventional?' Max tossed the pills into his mouth, took a gulp of water and threw back his head, grimacing as they slid down his throat. 'What you are suggesting is childish.' *Childish,* isn't that exactly what his father had thrown in his face when, as a young boy, he'd first shown him his sketches. 'If this got out to my competitors,' he said, forcing his mind from a memory he vowed never to revisit, 'can you imagine what it would do to my reputation?'

'Not nearly as damaging as being paralysed by a stroke and having to be spoon-fed, Sophia snapped. 'And since when have you cared what others think? Besides, you have an island on the other side of the world.

'One you've been too busy to visit. Fiji is remote enough for you to step away from the constant flash of cameras and be virtually anonymous,' she said, lowering her voice as Max's new PA cat-walked into his office. 'Call yourself Mr. Johnstone, or Mr. Smith, or whatever else you want, to protect your privacy.'

Beneath long-fringed lashes the PA gave Max a sultry look, trailing her gaze over his lean and muscled form, as she placed a collection of fashion magazines and media cuttings in a neat pile precisely as she'd been trained.

'Thank you, that will be all,' Sophia said, dismissing her.

'A nudist camp would be vastly more appealing,' Max said. His gaze trailed after his PA as she left his office. While he had no time for relationships, that didn't stop him from appreciating beauty. How much easier it would be to lie naked amongst a bevy of loveliness than expose his feelings to the spotlight.

Sophia rolled her eyes. 'I can just imagine what that would do to your blood pressure. Art, unlike making a career of intimately studying the curves of women, my dear brother, is therapeutic.'

'So you want me to go to kiddy school and make a fool of myself.' Irritation coursed through his veins as he ran his fingers around the neck of his shirt and loosened the starched white collar.

'You never had a childhood,' Sophia said, her voice almost a whisper. 'You grew up too fast. We both did. And now you're a thirty-five-year-old man who may not see forty.'

'I know you are trying to help but I told you I can handle it.' And he would. He would never abandon his responsibility. Unlike his father who had tried to combine work with marriage and failed at both, Max had gladly sacrificed his personal life for his career.

Abandoned at birth by his biological parents, raised briefly by strangers, then dumped in a boarding school, he had turned what could have been a weakness into his biggest strength.

Self-reliance.

'All this stress has engulfed you, Max. Only you can't see it. And it scares me. You've become a shell of yourself—more than you were already. A man so cut off from his feelings that you are devoid of emotion. You've become a lighthouse of a man—lonely in a crowd, aloof and detached. Uncaring.'

The words bounced off Max's chest like the final shards of Milan's winter sun reflecting off the panoramic glass windows. It was true. He no longer cared.

'What do you want from me, Sophia?'

She paused, concern pooling in her dark eyes. 'I want what our mother wants. I want you to be happy.'

His lips curved in a tight mocking smile. When had his real mother ever cared about his happiness? He knew what she really wanted. After suddenly reappearing in his life, she wanted a daughter-in-law and she wanted a grandson. Max shook his head and gave a short exacerbated sigh. She wanted the impossible.

He plunged his hand through his hair, raking it back from his brow. He should have had it cut razor short last week. Instead, he'd thrown himself into the roll out of his retail network of 60 Massimilliano Balforni boutiques and jewellery stores throughout China, and the pending development of his luxury hotel in Dubai, with such single-minded, unrelenting focus there had been no time for indulgences.

'I've done my research,' he said, adding his signed consent to the final contracts, 'and from every angle it all seems based on spurious psychology.' His hand closed around the pen as he looked up sharply.

Sophia sucked her breath as though steeling herself to battle with his formidable will. 'Unless you make some changes, and I mean massive changes,' Sophia glanced momentarily in the direction of Cimitero Maggiore, Milan's largest cemetery, then fixed Max with a penetrating gaze, 'you'll end up like our father. *Morte.*'

'That will not happen to me,' he said, balling his fingers into a fist. 'I am nothing like our father.'

'No, you're not. You are loyal, honest and immensely generous to the people you care about—nothing like our father. But you are an unrelenting workaholic like he was. No better than an addict, because despite all your willpower, all your determination, all your talent, all your wealth you can't stop working. My God, you even live above your office.'

'*Mia sorella,* even if I wanted to go finger painting, which I do not, there is no way I can get away. People need me. I cannot just walk away without everything collapsing.'

'Even geniuses need time out to replenish. Super-heroes too,' she laughed. 'You, Clark Kent, need a rest from being Superman, a week out of this world. Not eternity. I will take care of things until you're back.'

The blood vessel in his temple pulsed, whether out of conviction or rebellion he didn't know, but her suggestion was not without merit. His sister had proven herself capable in so many ways since her appointment to Director of Public Relations.

He leaned back in his chair, steeping his fingers against his lips as he savoured a compelling idea. What if he could achieve several goals by leaving Italy? While he did not believe in fate, he did believe in destiny. Was it not destiny after all that had led him to this career, launching him from male model to CEO of a multi-billion dollar empire?

Max began to wonder if his recent conversation with some Fijian silk merchants was also pre-destined. Until that meeting he hadn't known there was such a large population of Indians in Fiji, and he'd been intrigued by the innovative textile developments they had shared with him.

And he could maximise efficiencies by going undercover and checking out his hotel chain in the Pacific. Yes, he thought, warming to the idea, perhaps a change of scene, getting away from all things European might just revive his flagging spirits.

His creativity was blocked, young designers were licking at his heels. He needed to continually innovate, but nothing inspired him. The plan was worth considering after all. Nothing else had worked. Plus it would get Sophia off his case. And the art therapy gimmick she was so convinced he needed?

What could any dowdy art therapist do to him that he couldn't control?

3

'First time to Fiji?' the porter asked art therapist Issy Riley as they wove past the rows of poolside loungers. Bronzed men and women wearing barely-there swimsuits tanned their lithe bodies beneath the last rays of the sun.

Issy was by far the most uniquely dressed, she thought euphemistically, gazing beyond the pool to the azure sea, fringed with coconut trees. Some, no doubt, would argue she was, in fact, the worst-dressed person at the resort, but then she'd never cared for fashion.

She pushed up the sleeves of the yellow shaggy pile of her jumper as two women sauntered past, tanned from crown chakra to pink toenails, their double d-cups jiggling like caramel panacottas.

Surrounded by an ocean of virtual nakedness Issy felt prudish dressed head-to-toenails in winter discomfort. Certainly less chic than the five-year old meandering past, resplendent in streaming caftan and matching overly bejewelled sandals, snapping the sunset with her iPhone.

'Yes. First time anywhere overseas, actually,' she ran her

fingers over the roll of her turtleneck, wishing she'd thought to wear a tee-shirt so she could peel the jumper off.

As always she'd left things too late. She'd been in a mad panic to get to the plane and hadn't even thought to pack spare clothes to change into once she'd arrived at Nadi airport.

Taking refuge beneath a palm tree Issy momentarily relaxed as a choir of Fijian men and women dressed in flowing white gowns began to sing in the open area just beyond the pool. Their voices soared through the humid air. Then suddenly realising they were singing Christmas carols tension knotted her shoulders.

Christmas.

When she'd offered to help her business partner Nancy, and take this last minute client, Issy had thought she could escape the festive season, dripping with tinsel and baubles, and the promise of happiness.

Her fingers tightened around the note the receptionist had passed her when she'd checked in. At least work meant she wouldn't have to spend the holiday season at her mother's with HIM—the traitorous, lying, three-timing control-freak of a fiancé. Make that ex-fiancé, she corrected. She had dumped him the moment she discovered his betrayal, but that didn't stop her heart from taking a hit.

Issy stared into the distance her attention diverted by a huge Christmas tree blazing with a rainbow of coloured lights. She closed her eyes and sighed. Why couldn't she find a promise-keeper?

Married by Christmas? Nope. Once again the bus of happily-ever-after failed to pull up at her stop, but to find out on Facebook that James was cheating on her weeks before their wedding? No one deserved that humiliation.

Even if her mother still thought James was the best thing

since sliced toast, at least Issy had the balls to shut down his lies, the courage to confront the truth, the strength to face life on her own again. She swallowed hard as the sharp edge of betrayal ran a ragged line through her chest. She'd had a lucky escape.

The porter smiled stiffly as though sensing her discomfort. 'Holiday?' he asked.

Issy looked longingly at people relaxing by the pool, her gaze hovering over a loved-up couple entwined on a sun-lounger. She felt a tug of disappointment. Would she ever trust enough to fall in love again? She crushed the note from her client in her hands, pressing her lips together as she turned away. 'Business.' she said.

All the men in her life, even her father, had let her down terribly. Work was a most welcome distraction. She didn't need a man in her life, she reminded herself. Not anymore.

A riot of shouts from the beach pulled her attention toward a group of men jabbing at something writhing on the sand at the edge of the lagoon. Whether it was an instinctive sense of brutality etched in the men's postures or the impact of the powerful figure brushing past her, she didn't know, but every whisper of her body hair stood erect.

Issy watched mesmerised, adrenaline lapping her body as a 6 foot 3 Adonis with olive toned six-pack abs and a body that could easily grace a billboard strode toward the men. He was clad only in tiny trunks.

He looked strangely familiar in an unfamiliar sort of way, like a celebrity in a magazine, the same handsomeness, and aloof assurance, although she knew she'd never met him before. He looked like a movie star. Certainly not a man anyone would forget.

His muscles rippled gold fire under the heat of the fading tropical sun as, with powerful, lithe steps like a panther about to lunge, the titan advanced upon the men on the beach. Fear shadowed their faces as they turned to each other, eyes widening, aware this was no normal man approaching but a warrior, a leader of men, a man not to be defied.

'*Allora*! Stop!' His rich honey-toned voice, edged with a deep sultry Italian accent, sent shivers coursing through her body.

Tearing her eyes away from the perfect specimen of a man Issy perched on her toes, squinting under the bright sun to see what the titan was so vigorously trying to protect.

'Sea snake. Very poisonous,' the porter said.

Danger.

The warning flashed red in her mind and jackknifed through the air. Was it the snake she was afraid of or the rush of molten emotion the stranger incited?

'Come and see,' the porter beckoned.

She hesitated, torn between fear and fascination. Her pulse hammered, pummelled by the unexpected handsome-ness of the man and stricken with curiosity. What sort of person would go to a snake's rescue?

For the first time in forever she felt excited, alive, her body on edge, ablaze. Why, when she was officially off men, and as she walked toward him did every whisper of hair on her body stand alert?

She frowned, trying to remember any man ever having inflamed such a reaction, as his muscular arms took the sticks from the assailants. Arms that could crush an opponent or protect a woman against his powerful lean body.

'We're only trying to protect the resort guests from danger,' the men shouted.

'*Che cavolo*! Can you not see the baby snake?' he jabbed his finger towards the rocks. 'Would you deprive her of its mother?' His eyes were a lethal shade of gunpowder blue, his gaze unyielding, freezing the men in a chilly silence. 'She will not strike unless provoked.'

Issy's breath caught in ragged gasps as she glanced at the tiny snake lingering in the distant shadows. Was this guy for real? Someone like her, who cared nothing for the senseless killing of animals.

'We didn't see it. We didn't think,' they said, stepping back. 'Sorry, Sir.'

Issy smiled, her body flooded with something that felt uncomfortably like admiration. She dragged her eyes from the Italian god and focused on the snake lying washed ashore, exposed in its vulnerability.

As dangerous as the snake was alleged to be the artist in her was captivated by the beauty of its iridescent pearl and obsidian stripes. But she was wary too, of its potent power. Was the snake feigning death or was it spellbound, against its will, offering herself to the giant of a man before her?

Issy's heart seemed to freeze then pounded like the sea crashing on the distant reef. She could relate to feeling out of her depth. She stole a glance at the knight without armor standing in far too skimpy trunks as with soft, deft movements that belied his powerful physique, he gently nudged the snake toward the sea.

Issy kept her gaze firmly on the snake as it uncoiled slowly, writhing in the wet sand as Issy drew closer to its rescuer. She stood a body's length away from him, agonisingly aware of the rich lustre of his full head of blue-black wavy hair, his impeccably shaven jaw, and the intoxicating aroma of his cologne coiling through the balmy air. Earthy, sensual, exhilarating.

What was up with that, she wondered bamboozled by the commotion clanging through her mind. Her eyes recklessly savoured every contoured edge of the Adonis's body as he stood at the water's edge watching the snake slither to freedom.

She traced his broad, bronzed, well-oiled chest, before sliding down the tantalisingly playful coils of soft dark hair dividing his sculptured six pack and marching a confident line from his navel, before vanishing below the rim of his tiny 'spray on' trunks.

Suddenly the Adonis turned toward her and she was immediately captured in the web of his intense blue eyes.

Issy looked away quickly. Too quickly.

Sprung!

Her face flamed carmine red as she studied her feet, wishing the escaping waves of rose pink hair that fell over her face as she did so would hide her indefinitely. After a brief moment she glanced up, hoping he had not read her mind when she'd gawked at him. The smirk on his face and the intensity of his gaze left her in no doubt he'd registered her attraction.

'Thank you for saving the snake Mr Johnstone,' said the porter, offering him a towel as he went to his side.

'Johnstone?' her voice eked out. Her eyes ping-ponged between the stranger and the porter. Thrusting her hand in her pocket, she unfurled the note the receptionist had given her. Issy's stomach dived a nervous somersault that would have done an Olympic swimmer proud. She reread the message, studying the words forged in firm, confident handwriting—no sign of weakness anywhere. "Meet me by the pool. (Signed) Mr. Johnstone."

Oh, God. Mortification coiled through her body. 'You can't be *that* Mr. Johnstone.'

He stared at her as if she was insane.

She bit her lip, holding back any attempt at an explanation

for her earlier behaviour that she knew would only dig a deeper hole.

'There must be some mistake.'

Did you enjoy reading this excerpt?
*A*vailable now, in audio, paperback and eBook

Claimed
By The Sheikh
MOLLIE
MATHEWS

CLAIMED BY THE SHEIKH

THE SHEIKHS UNTAMED BRIDES

MOLLIE MATHEWS

CLAIMED BY THE SHEIKH

BOOK TWO IN THE TRUE LOVE SERIES.

Available now

A grief-stricken Sheikh Tariq na Hassir, the formidable ruler of the Kingdom of Avana, arrives in Paris to claim his brother's child after a car crash killed his parents--only to find out from the hospital that the child isn't their biological son. It's Tariq's son, with his former lover.

Three years ago, after being banished by Tariq from his desert kingdom, renown architect Melanie Jones secretly gave her baby to Tariq's childless brother and his wife, in a swap the world was never supposed to discover.

The tragedy pulls her back to the world that rejected her and the man who abandoned her—the only man capable of tuning her carefully controlled world upside down.

Tariq will do whatever it takes to protect his legacy, including claiming Melanie as his bride and his son as heir before scandals ensue. But Melanie has other plans for her future—a westernized life where she's free to operate her own business and control her own life.

Join Mollie's new release newsletter here http://eepurl.com/cigEsH. Be the first to know when *the next book in the series* is released.

NOTE FROM THE AUTHOR

Dear Friends,

I hope you enjoy *Claimed by the Sheikh*. It touches on a number of subjects I love and care about with the twists and turns in the plot. I always love celebrating the strength of the human spirit, and what people do when faced with seemingly insurmountable challenges in their lives, and how unexpected events can turn disaster or tragedy into something good.

I love the fact that Melanie follows an unusual path as a pioneering architect. I love how hard she works at it. I always enjoy exploring how each of us uses and expresses our particular talents. And I felt a bond with her, because I too studied architecture—but I didn't have the courage and determination that Melanie had to finish.

Watching Melanie struggle with discrimination, knock-backs, and success, and the price you pay for them, was familiar to me too. Each person lives success differently and her adventures along the way help her become the person she is destined to be. Whatever your path in life, you have a gift. Something nobody else can do as beautifully and skillfully as you.

How you express it, how you live it, and how you share it with others is unique to you. You have your own special way of dealing with life and the talents you've been given, whether you hide those gifts or share them openly.

I hope you enjoy reading about this talented young architect, and following her story as it unfolds. Victory and success come in many forms and guises, her path is an exciting, fascinating, and re- warding one, and I'm sure yours will be too!

With all my love,
Mollie

PRAISE FOR CLAIMED BY THE SHEIKH

"Wow, just wow, I can't articulate enough how compellingly page-turning this remarkable story was. If I could give it more than 5 stars this would be it! This author has the gift & the power to make you experience her remarkable craft on a whole other level. I was drawn into the story when she shared a few chapters with me quite a while ago now & I'm beyond thrilled that she managed to finish it. I'm not one to tell the story, the blurb & other reviewers will cover that but I will concede that this magical, mystical, hauntingly beautiful story will stay with me for the longest time. Highly recommended."

~ Terry Babb

"Claimed by the Sheikh was a fast paced read that held my interest from the first page to the last. The story had a depth to the characters and strong imagery due to the author's attention to details. Watching two worlds collide, as well as two strong characters fight for what they each believe is right, just added another layer to the story.

I enjoy books that are set in the desert with desert royalty or sheikhs. Claimed by the Sheikh was a strong story with a depth to the characters of both Tariq and Melanie who we get to know a little at a time as well as their history from three years before. They seem to have unresolved issues and feelings for each other but given their differences will it be any different this time around? There was very strong imagery due to the vivid descriptions of the scenery, the palace and Melanie's drawings, which made me feel that I was there. Tariq's rescue of endangered animals and his philanthropy was a nice addition to the story. I liked how the child, Salim, was brought into the story as well as his importance to the story line. Ms. Mathews is fast becoming a favorite author."

~ JoAnne

"This book grabbed me from the first page. Both lead characters were portrayed fully as real people not just by how they looked as in many books. There being a child involved added to my enjoyment!"

~ Melba

"The tone for this book is set in the opening chapters as the young Sheikh is faced with ongoing difficulties in the kingdom created by his atrocious father. He is fighting an ongoing battle to prevent himself from being sucked into the past and to rather create a new and prosperous future for his people. Tariq's previous rejection of Melanie and the results have soured her against romantic love and made her determined to carve a career for herself."

~ Margaret

"I really like the premise of the book, I always like the royal romance with impediments to happiness and this book has it in spades. I like the strong figure of the Sheikh and the strong heroine who has built a professional career. Immediately I can see lots of problems that seem insurmountable at first: their past stormy relationship, the baby secret, her desire to have her own career, his desire for an heir, his demand to raise the child, his vow to swear off women. I also like that, right of the bat, we learn about his plan to build a reserve for animals and to right the many wrongs from his father's legacy. These are all good foundations for a fiery, passionate and conflicting relationship."

~ Elaine

"Fantastic premise that has a substantial conflict behind it. I like Melanie a lot. A strong female heroine is what I want to read. I think that is particularly important with such a powerful man, and here in this instance, someone who can wield such power. I love love love the beginning. This is one tough guy but the book opens with him protecting a baby giraffe. Fantastic opening."

~Leanne

"Tariq's emotional conflict is that he is in love with Melanie and won't admit it to himself. As a reader, it keeps me on pins and needles to see if Tariq realizes it himself."

~ Tonni

"It hooked me, it was impactful and well written. Sexual tension is always a plus for me and I loved the strong characters."

~ Terry

"I wanted to keep reading. It was intriguing."

~Robyn

"Claimed by the Sheikh has an intriguing plot: keeping the Sheikh's illegitimate child a secret through all the complications that arise. The main characters, Melanie as the independent architect and Tariq as the wealthy, powerful Sheikh of a fictitious Arab country are well fleshed out and believable. You have empathy for their situation and the tension about whether the secrets will be revealed carries you through the book. This is the stuff of fairy tales. The book does go a long way towards helping the reader understand Tariq's Islamic beliefs and his commitment to helping his people and the endangered animals he wants to rescue. There is a nice subplot about Melanie's struggle to become recognized as a creative architect in a field dominated by men. Tariq's wealth comes in handy there. A good heartfelt romance."

~Elaine

PROLOGUE

The traffic on the motorway started to speed up as they got closer to Charlotte's husband's new office in the French headquarters of the Fédération Internationale de Football Association in southern France.

Salim was still asleep in the backseat when Charlie looked at her watch and realized it was nearly 1 am and they were going to be late to pick up Zayed. If he was exhausted, as he often was at the end of a long day, she knew he wouldn't wait. He had been working so hard rebuilding his life to provide for her and Salim. Tonight had been a special celebration. She was proud that he had won the election to be the new FIFA president. His campaign focused on change, football ideals and uniting warring countries through their common passion for sport. She didn't want to be late.

Charlie grabbed her iPhone from the dashboard and placed it in her lap, to send him a text, when Salim suddenly woke.

"Don't drive and text, Mommy!" he said, disapprovingly. "You'll cause an accident."

"I just want to tell Daddy that we're running a few minutes late, but we're almost there. Otherwise, he'll grab a ride with one of his staff and leave before we arrive." Charlie looked down and started texting quickly, holding the steering wheel firm with one hand.

Ten minutes later Salim saw his father first as they approached the building where he worked. "Daddy!"

Charlie pulled to the curb, got out of the car and opened the passenger door. Salim had already unbuckled his seatbelt and climbed out of his booster seat. He ran to his father.

Zayed scooped him into his powerful arms and drew Charlie to his side. His sheer strength and physicality always made her swoon and she leaned into his chest.

"*Marhabaan, habibti*. Hello, my love. How's my favorite team?" he said, placing a kiss on Charlie's lips before turning to Salim and kissing his chubby cheeks.

"You must be tired," Charlie said.

Zayed heaved a deep breath, sucking the early morning air into his lungs. "Exhausted!"

"I'll drive," Charlie said. "Why don't you sit in the back and take a nap? I don't want you to be too tired to give me some special attention when we get home," she laughed, planting a sloppy kiss on his sexy lips.

She was thinking about Melanie and how grateful she was to her sister as she embraced Salim and Zayed. She wanted to take a selfie of them and send her a text but they agreed not to stay in contact. Those were the rules. Besides they had their own busy lives in separate worlds. She wasn't obliged to call, but she wanted to. But she didn't want to upset her or retraumatize her sister either. It wouldn't be fair to her. Not when Charlie was so happy, and Melanie was all alone. *Without Salim.*

Charlie swallowed back the little trace of guilt that she never managed to kick and smiled as she watched Zayed clamber into the car, curling his long-powerful frame like a contortionist, into the back. He waited for Salim to climb in and rested his head against the booster seat and fell asleep.

She was so happy. She didn't need to be a princess. She didn't need Zayed's royal title. All she needed was her two favorite men, she thought as she pressed the keyless start and pulled out from the curb.

Charlie wanted to get home quickly. Both her boys needed to be in their beds. She hadn't wanted to leave Salim with a babysitter and was feeling a little reprehensible for lifting him from his warm bed to pick up his dad, but she knew how much Zayed had missed them both. He had been working so hard and tonight had been a well-earned celebration. Thankfully their home was only a fast 40 minute trip on the A7 autoroutes du Soleil.

They hadn't traveled far when Salim's eyes suddenly fluttered open. "You're not wearing your seatbelt!" he censured.

Charlie glanced at him in the rear-view mirror and noticed that Salim and Zayed weren't buckled in either. She'd heard the chime but had been distracted, worrying about Melanie, and how she must be suffering. She'd been rushed and stressed all day.

"Neither are you," Charlie said, turning around.

"I forgot, mommy," Salim said, he rubbed his sleepy eyes and started to put his seatbelt on, but it was caught in the door and he couldn't. He tugged and pulled on it. "It's stuck, mommy."

Charlie's heart raced as she turned to keep her eyes on the road. She was sitting right on the legal speed limit of 80 mph. It always felt so fast. Behind and in front of her was a line of other cars and there was no room to pull over. She couldn't stop now, without causing an accident.

"We'll be home in a minute, darling," she said, glancing at Salim again in the rear view mirror. The words had barely left her mouth when his eyes flew wide in horror. He saw a huge tourist bus careering toward them from the left.

PROLOGUE (CONT.)

Salim screamed. Charlie turned too late. The bus hit them with monstrous force.

Zayed woke and hurled his body across his son instinctively.

There was the sound of crushing metal and splintering glass as Charlie's cellphone flew from her hand. Salim watched in horror as his mother shot through the windshield like a torpedo. She careered through the air, and disappeared under the cars in front. Their SUV struck another, stopped abruptly, and Salim and his father were crushed amongst a mangled heap of other cars.

The bus had shunted them three lanes over. The driver lay motionless with his head on the steering wheel as people rushed from their cars toward him, and several others ran toward Charlie's car.

The sky was ablaze with tiny lights from their cellphones as people were calling the emergency services. A crowd were staring at Charlie under the vehicle where she had landed, covered with blood and broken glass. Traffic was backed up behind them, and within minutes sirens screamed in the distance. People wandered dazed and numb with shock as they surveyed the carnage.

The driver of the bus was concussed and staggered from the wreck, but there was no sign of life under the car where Charlie had landed. Salim lay beneath his father's powerful body, his head, face, and arms covered with blood. No one dared touch Salim or Zayed for fear of injuring them further. No one knew if they were alive. As they waited for the emergency services to arrive it looked hopeless. But there was so much blood and twisted metal everywhere, no one could see clearly.

A paramedic team arrived by helicopter. The crew pulled Salim and Zayed from the wreckage.

Zayed was pronounced dead and Salim was immediately assessed as in a critical condition. They inserted a breathing tube before they left the scene and airlifted him to a hospital in Montpellier with life-threatening head injuries. More paramedics and emergency services arrived, including an ambulance, sirens shrieking and lights flashing,

They removed Charlie and Zayed's body from the scene. It was hours before traffic began, moving again. In total, two people were dead, and eight people had been injured but none severely except Salim. The police and paramedics had said Zayed had died instantly when his skull was crushed against the hard surface of the television in the backseat of the car. When Charlie was thrown through the windshield and hit the pavement, she had died on impact. It was a tragedy made less horrific by knowing death had come instantly and they hadn't suffered.

The police found a blue backpack with an image of Simba from the movie The Lion King, and a soft toy of Simba too, on the floor of the car. The backpack had a name badge with Salim's name on it, and Charlie's purse with her driver's license was crushed in the front passenger seat, together with her cellphone. The screen was shattered but they could still see the picture of Charlie, Zayed, and Salim smiling on the home-screen.

Charlie and Zayed were taken to the morgue by the police. There was nothing in Charlie's purse or Zayed's wallet listing next of kin or who to notify in an accident. All they knew, for now, were their names and that they weren't French.

The paramedics had assessed that Salim had a serious head injury, a broken arm, and probably internal injuries. The police noted that none of them had been wearing seatbelts. All the police could deduce was that Charlie hadn't seen the oncoming bus, and possibly had been on her cellphone or texting. Both were common causes of accidents and fatalities. Beyond that, they knew nothing not even whether Salim would survive the accident. It looked unlikely when they'd left the scene and flew at full speed to Montpellier Hospital.

1

———

"Are you trying to kill her?" Tariq na Hassir, the formidable ruler of the Kingdom of Avana, seized the animal handler's arm, forcing him to release the rope laced around the baby giraffe's neck.

"She has suffered enough trauma." Tariq dismissed the man with a fierce scowl that stuck fear into enemies.

A slither of panic crept into the young man's hushed apology. "I am sorry your Excellency."

"Release the others from their cages," Tariq growled.

The man did not have to be asked twice. He knew from experience that the Sheikh's retribution for disobedience would be swift and merciless.

"You are safe from harm," Tariq said softly, stroking the baby giraffe's long neck with a gentleness that belied his strength.

"No one will ever hurt you again, Noor," he said softly, impulsively naming her as his fingertips swept through the calf's fur. He let his long supple fingers linger a moment upon her tail. Thankfully they had saved her in time, he thought as he reached for the reins, clenching his powerful hands around the soft leather.

The rage he had first felt on hearing about the ruthless murder of the new born's mother still roared through him. Had she been executed to pay a tail dowry to the father of some money-mongering bride, he wondered? Or did some heinous person pay thousands of dollars for a wretched fly swatter?

Noor looked up and met Tariq's dark gaze. In her innocent eyes, he saw her despair, her disillusionment, her disgust with humanity. He recognized her trauma as though it was his own. Because it was.

"Humans," he said, his voice marinated with contempt. "The people you should be able to trust, the people who say they care, the people whose actions should be driven by love —the majority are driven by nothing but selfishness, deception, and lies."

Taking a bottle of milk, he placed the teat to Noor's lips. The calf's silky black lashes grazed her cheeks as she gazed down at the foreign object then looked back at Tariq. She stared silently up at him, her eyes moist and bewildered.

Tariq had trained himself to shut down his emotions but that skill suddenly failed him. His chest trembled with suppressed rage knowing the orphaned baby would never again taste her mother's milk.

"What passes for love among some people is abhorrent," he said in a low, strained voice. "On behalf of humanity, I apologize."

The killing of the calf's mother and three other rare Kordofan giraffes by trophy hunters seeking their tails further motivated the Sheikh's commitment to transform his anger into action.

"Do you really think you can save her?"

Tariq looked at Anwar, his younger brother by 11 months. His head was slightly bowed but he could see his eyes were fixed in sadness and longing.

Tension ripped down Tariq's spine. "Our father's reign of terror and tyranny have robbed Avana of prosperity and peace. I will make it my personal mission to right the injustices of the past. War and hostility must end. And it starts with how we treat those most vulnerable."

His fingers shook as he gripped the bottle of milk as Noor, at last, began to suckle.

An eerie silence swept across the precipitous landscape of Avana's Tiwa oasis. Tariq lifted his gaze to the horizon. The only movement visible to his naked eye was the wind etching a delicate furrow as it crawled over the golden dunes.

"Not only will I provide a sanctuary for hunted wildlife and orphans like Noor, but I will liberate God's most precious creatures from the many closing zoos and other inhumane habitats around the world," he glanced over at the other animals being unloaded from the custom-built crates.

"I will create a world-acclaimed sanctuary, impenetrable by those with impure and malicious hearts. It will be the most magical, marvelous, mesmerizingly unique place, the number one eco-tourism destination in the world. I will create meaningful employment for our people, restoring their dignity, attracting millions of visitors annually and contributing billions to the economy. But more importantly, I will show the world how kindness and compassion can be turned into plutonium and change the world."

Anwar glanced at the now lush landscape and recalled how barren it had once been. With no sign of life in sight, others had found it impossible to fathom his brother's vision to transform the punishing and unforgiving conditions into a haven for so many endangered species. Yet, as with everything Tariq turned his formidable will and mind-blowing wealth to, he had succeeded where mere mortals were destined to fail.

Anwar's heart swelled with pride as he thought of all his brother's achievements. "It's an audacious and admirable plan. And if anyone can pull it off it's you, brother. Your passion, your drive, your unrelenting ambition and pursuit of goals exceeds mere mortals. And you have the endurance and power of 13,000 Arabian horses, but aren't you setting yourself up for too much hard work? Why don't you relax? Kick back. Enjoy the fruits of your reign?" Anwar said, tossing his head in the direction of the harem. "Other men would."

"Women were our father's weakness," bitterness bled from his words. "I too once made the same mistake. I too paid the price."

There was a tense silence while Tariq lifted his gaze to the sky and studied the giant falcon circling above.

"Was it not you who once taught that your greatest weakness can also be your greatest strength?" Anwar asked.

Tariq shook his head, biting down a terse retort. "I was misled." He said, nodding his command to the animal handler lingering at a respectful distance.

He petted Noor as she was led away. "All kinds of atrocities are committed in the name of love, which is why it is the most dangerous of emotions, and why I am forever turned off to women."

2

<hr>

Shielding his eyes from the blazing sun, Tariq looked skyward, honing in on the falcon's intense, focused gaze. The power, the force, the courage and the vision of the hunting dog of the sky inspired him. And unlike humans falcons were loyal—a quality Tariq valued above all else.

"The best time for a man is the time he spends with his family," he said, glancing toward his brother. "My people are my family. My animals are my family. You are my family," he said, patting his brother's shoulders.

"The first responsibility of a leader is to make his people happy and then to provide them with the required security, stability, comfort, progress and development to ensure their survival. My loyalty is to you all."

Tariq's head jerked backward sharply as he recalled the brutal tyranny of his father. "Besides what sort of man doesn't want to care for his family? Only an ego-driven tyrant like our father would turn a blind eye to the plight of our people and the cruelty imposed on God's creatures."

Tariq gritted his teeth, his jaw locking against the strain of suppressing his emotions. There was no point voicing the hostility he felt toward his father. There was no purpose in reminding his brother that his father was a behemoth, a beast, a toxic mix of oppressiveness and evilness who had wielded monstrous power and made their lives a misery.

"This has to be the most isolated place in the world," Anwar muttered, gazing out forlornly at the neutrals and as-far-as-the-eye-can-see block tones of the desert. "No wonder mother fled to London."

While Tariq missed his mother deeply he didn't share his brother's despair. He was a thirty-six-year-old ruler who was pouring his power, his infinite wealth, his heart and soul into the land and the animals who he now offered sanctuary. He was a king filled with purpose.

"There is a lot of anti-Islamic sentiment in the world. People believe we are a nation of murderers. Thanks to people who corrupt our ways for their evil agenda. Thanks to our father and his violent, corrupt rule. Thanks to warlords and governments who seek to profit from war and spread their lies. Because of all these things the international community fears us. They have been driven away. I want to bring people back here. I want to restore our nation's pride. I want to show the world the beauty and kindness of true Islam. Our people have suffered enough shaming and violence."

"Again, you have set yourself a formidable task. Are you sure you're not throwing yourself into this audacious cause just to forget about your disobedient wife?"

"My ex-wife," he corrected. His brief marriage had been a disaster. He should have resisted the arrangement. He should have refused to cement his father's power-base by marrying the daughter of his pugnacious uncle.

Loyalty. That was Tariq's weakness. Loyalty, to family, no matter the personal cost.

The marriage was as archaic as it was disastrous. But that

didn't stop Tariq wanting a family—one that didn't place demands on him he wasn't equipped to keep.

Duty—that's what counted.

The irony didn't escape him. Duty had claimed his marriage. He knew Fatima took other lovers, just like he knew that some people weren't suited to marriage. But he also knew that if he hadn't been more married to his people and his quest than he'd ever been to his wife, he might have prevented her from escaping in the night with his bodyguard in a run-down-old jeep. He might have prevented her from being buried in the sandstorm that led to her death.

He gazed out at the stark, undulating desert landscape. If he had to atone for his sins, he'd rather do it out here where there was nothing but the eerie silence and the hot wind surfing over the dunes. Where there was nothing other than his rescued wildlife meandering over what felt like the plains of the Serengeti. Where there was nothing but the blazing desert, the sand beneath his toes, and the endless Arabian sea cutting them off from the world.

Duty required sacrifice.

Tension knotted his gut as his mind drifted to the woman who angered him most. *Melanie Jones.* It had been her fault his older brother, Zayed had abdicated, and Tariq had been catapulted into the role of ruler.

Tariq vowed long ago that while he loved his older brother dearly, his disloyalty had cost too high a price. He had vowed, no matter how painful, he would never speak or think of them again.

Tariq ran his fingers down the dark brown back feathers of the hawk. "He who wants to advance should always look ahead," he said, turning to his younger brother.

"There are worse things than an eternity spent in this

beautiful kingdom of islands, miles away from anything, draped in wind and quiet, sandstorms and hot desert breezes. Anchored between the majestic desert and surrounded by the shimmering Arabian sea. You will understand the preciousness of this gift soon enough, Anwar."

The Kingdom of Avana had been the crown in the jewel of Tariq's ancestors since time began. Only this time, under his rule, instead of bloody and catastrophic wars provoked by his father's oppressive regime the Kingdom of Avana would enjoy a reign of prosperous peace.

And he'd dedicate himself to his cause—and none other. Because when he looked around Tariq didn't see the life-sentence his younger brother Anwar imagined or the choke-hold his older brother Zayed felt.

He saw his home.

Yet, while he wasn't given to despair he could see his future as well as anyone if he continued alone. Today's reclusive hermit is tomorrow's bitter, old relic, he told himself, as the falcon left his arm and flew toward the object of his ardent desire.

As he watched as the giant bird of prey courted a female falcon with acrobatic displays of daring aerial feats, he was acutely aware that a kingdom wasn't a kingdom with only a king to rule. To avoid Avana falling into the clutches of his father's tyrannical offspring he needed an heir.

The possibility was as outrageous as it was urgent. To bear an heir he needed a wife. The whole idea was impossible. Once betrayed, a thousand times wiser, he reminded himself.

His dark brows curved into a frown as he saw his bodyguards gallop on horseback away from the towering walls of the palace toward him.

His body tensed with the stillness of a wild animal whose every sense was alert, suspicious and wary as they approached.

"Your Excellency! Come quickly. There's been an accident."

3

"Please, please, please choose me," Melanie Jones prayed inwardly. She swallowed hard, an ache building in her chest, as she checked her watch, then checked again as she paced the floor outside the Council administrative offices in central London. She heaved a deep breath as her thoughts raced.

Six minutes until her fate would be decided. She checked her watch again. Five minutes, 59 seconds until the officials from The Council and the other key teams assessing her architectural design for the new community library would decide her fate.

Had she done a good enough job to convince them to sign off her concept for the project? The newly elected bureaucrats in the state government had challenged her design and costings, and the whole concept was in danger of coming to a crashing end.

Had she conceded too much when she yielded to their demands to rein in her vision?

Just for once she wished she could shrug off the stigma

that dogged her when time after time, despite her award-winning designs, none of her buildings were ever constructed.

Just once she wished the vision she saw, the beauty she visualized, the joy she knew would be felt by those who eventually inhabited her buildings, was shared by those with access to the vault of money needed to bring her designs into reality.

If she could just get the dammed bureaucrats to say 'yes'. Until then she'd be nothing but a paper architect. Her life's work nothing but drawings and dreams.

Dreams.

Melanie rubbed her temple, erasing the one dream she had promised herself to forsake. *She was not going to think of him.*

Her ebony-black brows knitted in a fierce line as she forced her mind to the task at hand. She glanced down at the scatter of sketches splayed across the boardroom desk, feeling a mix of awe and pride—and aloneness.

Despite the fact that her design was breath stompingly beautiful, and searingly exquisite, her concept was also daringly innovative. The sweeping feminine curves confronted many people's sense of what architecture was and what it wasn't.

While she did everything in her power to minimize her own feminineness, in her designs aggressive masculine lines, straight edges and harsh corners were resolutely banished.

Dispelled were the sharp, angular lines and boxy shapes that so many in her field admired for their cost efficiencies. Eradicated were the shapes and forms that looked more like watchtowers in the worst of the concentration camps. Welcomed were the soaring sweeps and sensuous curves that inspired and nurtured and united people regardless of race, gender, or belief.

Melanie slid her palms over the stiff folds of her shapeless noir-black upside-down jacket. The touch of tarpaulin did an adequate job of disguising her generous breasts, but even this wouldn't detract from what many considered to be her biggest failing.

She was a woman. A woman competing in a man's world.

People, she knew only too painfully, didn't like breaking with tradition. And they didn't like change. And they most definitely didn't like a woman telling them what to do.

Everyone had told her that convincing these officials as with all other decision-makers she had to influence would take more than skill and strength of purpose. She was the outsider, just as her buildings were. On the edge, confronting other people's notions of compliance and predictability and subservience.

She'd stayed late at her office working through the night as she always did. She was quietly confident, but it was an audacious design. Why couldn't she do what her mother had always told her to do—why couldn't she settle for less?

The community library was the biggest project she and her small team of fledgling architects had ever handled—and the most important. Books changed lives. Books made people better citizens. Books liberated people from their constrained lives.

Liberation. Freedom. Escape. She owed it to people. Her architecture was designed for everyday men and women—not the elite.

She had worked on the concept tirelessly, sacrificing the rest of her life. Architecture was her big love. *Her only love.* Work kept her guilt, and her anger and her shame at bay, she told herself ignoring the emptiness and longing that slopped in her belly, calling her a liar.

. . .

CLAIMED BY THE SHEIKH, book two in the True Love series series available now from all good bookstores.

ABOUT THE AUTHOR

MOLLIE MATHEWS writes fun, sophisticated, passion-filled contemporary romance. She is known for her "sensual, beautiful, empowered stories enveloped in true romance" (5-star review). Her books have resonated with a global audience. She has been featured in magazines, television, and radio.

A former child and family therapist Mollie passionately believes in the power of romance to transform people's lives. She loves Mother Theresa's words, *"We are all pens in the hands of a writing God sending love letters to the world."*

Her stories are unashamedly positive, optimistic, full of fun and passion.

She is graduate of Victoria University, in Wellington, New Zealand and has given keynote speeches at romance writers conventions and international seminars.

Mollie follows the sun, dividing her time between New Zealand and exotic locations—wherever she intends setting her next romance novel. She lives with her very own romantic hero, Lorenzo—tall, dark, terribly handsome and fluent in Spanish!

Follow her on BookBub https://www.bookbub.com/authors/mollie-mathews and on her blog https://www.molliemathews.com/category/blog/ and sign up for Mollie's newsletter at www.Molliemathews.com and receive her FREE gift.

BY MOLLIE MATHEWS

GEMSTONE BILLIONAIRE BRIDES:

THE ITALIAN BILLIONAIRE'S CHRISTMAS BRIDE

THE ITALIAN BILLIONAIRE'S SCANDALOUS MARRIAGE

GEMSTONE BILLIONAIRES 2 BOOK-BUNDLE BOX SET

GEMSTONE BILLIONAIRES 3 BOOK-BUNDLE BOX SET

PASSION DOWN UNDER:

MARRIED BY CHRISTMAS
BRIDE OF GOLD

TRUE LOVE:

FLIGHT of PASSION
CLAIMED by THE SHEIKH

***PASSION DOWN UNDER SASSY SHORT
     STORIES:***

TWIST OF FATE
LOVE ME FOREVER
LOVE ME AS I AM
FOREVER AND ALWAYS
THE LIGHTKEEPER'S LOVER
*PASSION DOWN UNDER 2 BOOK-BUNDLE
     BOX SET (Books 1 & 2)*
*PASSION DOWN UNDER 3 BOOK-BUNDLE
     BOX SET (Books 1, 2 & 3)*

PRAISE FOR MOLLIE MATHEWS

"A good read that takes you away to a tropical island to experience the steamy heat of two people determined to stay single in case they get hurt again. Max, a sexy, jaded Italian multi-billionaire meets up with Issy, a playful children's art therapist who has recently found out her fiancé was having an affair. Although I was initially skeptical as I usually go for historical romances, I'm glad I trusted my friend's recommendation because this book was delightfully compelling. The emotional vulnerabilities and character quirks combined with the sexual tension kept the pages turning. A frisky novel to curl up on the couch with or take away on your next trip."

~ Pauline Roberts

"This was a fun read I really enjoyed. It's perfect for a lazy weekend. This is the first book I have read by this author but it won't be last. I can't wait to be more."

~ Poppy

"Beautifully written. The author's vivid and descriptive writing style pulled me into a world I never wanted to leave. I loved the connection of art between two very different people and the healing it brought them both. A Very beautiful story!"

~ Hugh Harrison

"I joined Max to make the slow journey from betrayed broken-hearted individuals to the trusting and loving couple they become. Molly Mathew's writing transports you to places she is describing where you can kick back and relax for a while as this endearing story unfolds. Her characters soon become visible through her careful picture-building. Readers will like the Kiwi vernacular Issy invoices every now and then, and I think readers will enjoy getting to know the strong characters and the beautiful islands we're visiting. The author also tucks in some great life advice for everyone telling in the telling of this charming story. I hope you enjoy this book, too. I did."

~ Alfie Rues

"I loved, loved, loved this book. An instantly gripping, compelling and fun read. Escapism at its best. I couldn't put the book down and read it in one night. With exotic back-drops like Italy and Fiji and passionate characters, it made the perfect holiday read. Can kindness thaw a cold-heart? That's the question Mollie Mathews poses in her book about second chances and learning to love again.

Issy is a funny, compassionate art therapist who wants to escape Christmas after her jerk of a fiancé cheated on her. Even though she only works with troubled children she agrees to take on a last minute client for her friend and business partner. What she doesn't know is her client is hunky fashion house CEO Massimilliano Balforni. Sparks fly and it's an attraction Max vows to deny. He doesn't want Issy and her colored pencils from bringing the wounds of his childhood to the light.

Mollie Mathews skillfully creates a gripping dynamic between Issy and Max that sensually blends their animosity with undeniable attraction making the tension soar. I definitely recommend this book."

~ Lauri

New Zealand

Visit www.molliemathews.com to read more about all our books and to buy them. You will also find features, author interviews and news of author events, and you can sign up for e-newsletters so that you're always first to hear about our new releases.

Join Mollie's Readers Group:

https://www.facebook.com/groups/323525616931811

❀ Created with Vellum